HIS CHRISTMAS
ANGEL

HIS CHRISTMAS ANGEL

BY

MICHELLE DOUGLAS

MILLS & BOON

Pure reading pleasure

First published in Great Britain 2007
Large Print edition 2008
Harlequin Mills & Boon Limited,
Eton House, 18-24 Paradise Road,
Richmond, Surrey TW9 1SR

© Michelle Douglas 2007

ISBN: 978 0 263 20041 6

Set in Times Roman 16½ on 18 pt.
16-0408-49386

Printed and bound in Great Britain
by Antony Rowe Ltd, Chippenham, Wiltshire

To Greg, who made it all possible
and never stopped believing.

And to Maggie, for the walks,
the coffee and the encouragement.

CHAPTER ONE

SOL slammed through the house and out of the back door to the veranda. Gripping the railing, he hauled in a breath. Then another. *Half an hour.* He'd been back half an hour and already he was dying to get out of here. Nothing had changed.

For Pete's sake, you'd think after ten years...

He rolled his shoulders, trying to ease the tension that had them wedged up tighter than double-lapped dovetail joints. His eyes swept across the backyard. What a mess. The fence needed mending, the lawn needing mowing, and the—

Cassie's tree.

His angry thoughts slammed to a halt. He squinted into the afternoon sun, but two giant oleanders on the other side of the fence prevented him from making out much of the house in the yard beyond. Did Cassie Campbell still live there?

Cassie Parker, he amended. She'd married ten years ago.

And had been widowed for eighteen months. Some things had changed.

He dragged a hand down his face. Cassie wouldn't live there now. She'd live in the centre of town with the rest of the Parkers. She didn't need to live on the outskirts any more. And since her mother had died…

An ache hollowed out his chest. He hadn't come back for the funeral. He hadn't come back for Brian's funeral either.

He stared hard at what he could see of the house and yard, trying to imagine someone else living there, but he couldn't. His gaze came back to the tree squatting in the corner. His lips curved upwards and the tension seeped out of him. Back then the only thing that had kept life bearable around here was Cassie Campbell.

Cassie Parker, he reminded himself, and his smile faded.

He clenched the veranda railing again. What

did he think he was doing? Trying to catch a glimpse of her? He had an insane urge to butt his head against a veranda post. He'd left all thoughts of Cassie behind ten years ago.

Yeah, right. Which is why you're craning your neck over her back fence with your tongue hanging out.

He made a frustrated noise in the back of his throat. It wouldn't even be her fence any more. He went to turn away when a leg dangled out of the tree—a long, lean, female leg. He blinked and shaded his eyes.

Cassie?

His breath hitched, but curiosity propelled him down the back steps and across the yard all the same. That was a damn fine leg, and he was real curious to see who lived in Cassie's old place now.

A mumbled half-smothered expletive drifted out of the tree as he drew near, and for some reason it made him grin. He quickened his step and, without waiting for his eyes to adjust to the shade, glanced up. The breath was punched out of him and a strange choked noise emerged from the back of his throat. He couldn't have uttered a single coherent sound if his life had depended on it.

Dancing violet eyes swung around to stare down at him. They raked across his face, then generous lips formed a perfect O. 'Good Lord, if it isn't Sol Adams, home for Christmas at last.'

Cassie Campbell!

His heart started to pump hard and fast. He swallowed. The sound rolled in the spaces beneath the tree, loud in the summer afternoon. 'Hey, Cassie,' he finally managed to get out.

'Hey, Cassie?' She rolled her eyes. 'After ten years that's all you can think to say?'

Then she smiled. Really smiled. Cassie had always put her whole heart into a smile. It outshone the hot summer sun. He blinked, but he couldn't look away. His groin ached. The entire surface of his skin tightened, as if he'd grown too big for it.

Her smile wavered. 'You didn't even say goodbye.'

Her soft words speared through him, and in that moment he'd never regretted anything more in his whole sorry life. If in this very instant he could go back ten years—

She grinned suddenly, and every thought in his head fled.

'Help me out here, will you, Sol?'

Help…? With…? Then he noticed the kitten clutched in her arms.

She bent down and handed it to him. 'Don't you let it go,' she warned, as she disappeared back along the branch. She returned with a second kitten that she promptly handed to him. Disappeared again. In a daze he took a third, until his arms were nothing but a wriggling, curling mass of kitten.

She grinned. 'It doesn't look as if you have a spare hand to offer the lady.'

Her skin had the look of soft pink rose petals, and Sol wanted to reach out and take her hand, help her down. Touch her. He wanted to know if she felt as cool and soft as she promised. He tried to rearrange the bundle in his arms but it kept changing shape.

'Don't you let those kittens get away, Sol Adams.'

'No ma'am,' he said weakly as she leapt down beside him. Her fragrance filled his nostrils. She smelt of something flowery, tropical, like frangipani. He wanted to bury his face against her neck and inhale.

'I've been jumping out of this tree for more years than I can count. Do you seriously think I need a hand?'

'You are wearing a skirt,' he pointed out. And it fitted her like a dream. It swished around her thighs as if dancing in joy because it was wrapped around Cassie Campbell.

Parker, he amended.

He reckoned he'd be pretty darn happy if he were wrapped around Cassie like that. He blinked at the thought. 'I—umm.' He cleared his throat. 'It could, uh, hamper your tree-jumping, is all. That's what I meant.'

She grinned and lifted the skirt and his eyes near bugged clean out of his skull. How the hell did she expect him to keep hold of an armful of kitten when she—

Bike shorts! He let his breath out in a whoosh. She was wearing bike shorts under the skirt.

Her eyes twinkled mischief before she dived to her knees by the fence and pushed a loose paling to one side. Another kitten, smaller than its siblings, poked its head through the gap. 'Well, come on, then,' Cassie patted her knee. 'We haven't got all day.'

Man, she wouldn't need to call *him* twice, Sol thought.

Without further ado, the kitten squeezed through the gap and flew straight to her lap. Sol didn't blame it.

Cassie picked the kitten up and rose to her feet. 'C'mon, then.' She hitched her head in the direction of Sol's back veranda and he followed in a daze. Once there she closed the little gate, popped her bundle on the floor, then plucked the kittens from his arms one by one to join it.

Sol glanced at them, then grinned. 'Jeez, Cassie, these are the ugliest batch of kittens to ever grace the earth.'

She drew herself up to her full height of five feet ten inches. 'Ugly?'

Sol was one inch over six feet. Most women

had to throw their heads back to look him in the eye. Cassie didn't.

He got a crick in his neck from kissing most women. He wouldn't get a crick in his neck from kissing Cassie.

As if she'd read that thought in his face, Cassie let her gaze drop to his lips and Sol held himself rigid. Nothing moved except the pupils of her eyes, dilating and contracting. Then she shook her head and stepped back, and Sol heard the soughing of the breeze in the trees again, and the wings of a flock of rosellas as they swooped through the yard and over the house.

'Ugly?' Cassie's voice was strong, dragging him back into the present. 'What would you know about the matter, Sol Adams? These kittens aren't ugly; they're beautiful.'

He made himself look at one. Boy, she was stretching the truth there.

'I love these kittens.' She hitched up her chin. 'And when you love something it's beautiful. So you keep your *ugly* comments to yourself.'

He glanced at the kittens again. Okay, maybe ugly wasn't the right word. Maybe—

Cassie seized the littlest one and pushed its face close up to his. 'Look at it,' she ordered. 'Can you seriously call that ugly?'

It mewed plaintively and he couldn't help it. He reached out a finger and ran it across the tiny head. 'It's cute,' he finally mumbled, when Cassie kept eyeing him with that ferocious glare. On the spur of the moment he cupped his hands around hers and rubbed his cheek against the kitten's fur. Cassie's skin felt warm and alive. 'I'm sorry. I didn't mean to laugh at something you love.'

Her eyes widened. Something arced between them. Something sweet and pure he couldn't put a name to. She stepped back and he let his hands drop.

'Hey, Alec,' she called through the back screen door.

Alec wheeled to the door. 'You're early, missy.'

Sol stared at Cassie. Early for what?

'I haven't come to see you.' She winked at Sol. 'But make yourself useful and bring us out some drinks. It's hot.'

Sol's jaw dropped.

'Get them yourself, you hussy. I'm in a wheelchair.'

'Don't go playing the invalid with me. You know how to drive that thing. I'm timing you,' she called back, settling herself in one of the two chairs that sat either side of a small table.

Sol glared at the screen door, then at Cassie. 'Since when have the two of you been so chummy?' This was Alec, the man who'd raised him. Not someone Cassie would usually laugh with or joke with. He scowled and lowered himself to the other chair. At least she wouldn't have ten years ago.

Violet eyes surveyed him across the table. She rested her chin on her hand and for a long moment she didn't speak. 'So…' she said at last. 'He finally talked you into it, huh?'

Her long dark plait had gone, replaced with a sleek bob that brushed her shoulders. When she moved a certain way a curtain of hair fell across her face, dark and shiny. His fingers itched to run through it, to find out if it were as—

He shifted, hoping he hadn't been staring. 'Talked me into…?'

'Coming home for Christmas.'

She frowned when he remained silent. 'He didn't?'

'No.'

She shot a glance at the door and sighed. 'He's his own worst enemy, you know?'

'What do you mean?'

'I mean he's been whingeing and moaning at me for months now that you never come home.' Her eyes started to dance. 'I told him it served him right. I told him if I was you I'd never come back either.'

That jerked him around. 'You didn't?'

'Yes, I did.' She folded her arms and lifted her chin. 'I told him he was a mean old man.'

She had. She would. Sol suddenly threw his head back and laughed. It shifted something inside him too long held in check. He glanced at her, and a surge of affection shot through him. Cassie might have changed her name, but she was doing what she'd always done—making bad situations not so bad, making them bearable.

Her smile faded. 'Now he's just a scared old man.'

'Scared?'

The back screen door slammed open and Alec wheeled out, a tray balanced on his lap. 'Mind my kittens,' Cassie warned. 'I've brought them for a visit.'

Alec grumbled, but kept his eyes fixed on the floor. He dumped a jug of iced water and two glasses on the table. Sol blinked. The jug contained slices of lemon and ice cubes. Surely Alec hadn't—?

'You're not joining us?'

'I'm watching the test match, as you well know, missy.'

'Well, don't let me keep you.'

Sol watched in amazement as a reluctant grin spread across Alec's face. He couldn't remember Alec smiling for…well, he guessed it'd be eighteen years.

'Watch your back around this one,' he told Sol. 'She's just as likely to stick the knife in and twist it as not.'

It was the longest sentence Alec had uttered in the last half an hour. Sol had been gone for ten years. *Ten years.* But when he'd walked through the front door Alec had glanced up and muttered, 'So you're back, then,' as if Sol had just returned from the corner shop.

He'd been tempted to walk back out and book into a motel.

'And don't you forget it.' Cassie laughed as Alec wheeled back inside. She poured out two glasses of water and pushed one towards Sol. 'He's getting better. He didn't bellyache at me about the kittens.'

'Why do you say he's scared?'

She frowned, as if he'd disappointed her. 'Wouldn't you be scared if you were dying, Sol?'

He stared back, speechless. Ice trickled down the collar of his shirt and dripped down his backbone.

Cassie's eyes widened, then her hand flew to her mouth. 'You didn't know?'

Nope. Nobody had bothered mentioning that.

'But isn't that why you're home? I thought you'd talked to Dr Phillips.'

'I did.' He dragged a hand down his face. 'All he said was Alec needed to go into the nursing home. And that he expected a spot to become available after Christmas.'

Air whistled between her teeth. 'Of all the spineless… Wait till I get hold of him. I'm sorry, Sol, I'd never have blurted it out like that if—'

'It's not your fault, Cassie.' It was his. He'd stayed away too long. Questions clamoured through him, but as a kitten used his leg as a scratching post one of the least pressing popped out of his mouth. 'What are you doing with all these kittens?'

'They're Christmas presents for my senior citizens.'

Who were her senior citizens? Water sloshed over the sides of his glass as he dropped it back to the table. 'Good God, you're not giving one to Alec, are you?'

'What do you think?' she snorted. 'Besides, you can't have pets at the nursing home.'

A hard ball settled in the pit of his stomach as he watched a kitten attack the shoelaces on one of her sneakers. A sneaker attached to a long, lean leg. His eyes travelled upwards. Man, did she have great legs or what? They were firm and shapely, as if she got enough to eat these days.

She hunched over and smoothed the skirt of her dress over her knees. 'You never called him Dad, did you? You always called him Alec.'

The huskiness of her voice hauled him back. His lips twisted as he met her gaze. 'Nobody could ever accuse Alec and me of being close, now, could they?'

'No,' she agreed. She ran a finger around the rim of her glass. Condensation gathered beneath it. 'He's changed, Sol.' Her finger stilled. 'He hasn't had a drink in two years.'

Was she serious? The hard ball in his stomach grew. Was it the drink that had made him sick? Why else would she…? 'What are you trying to say, Cassie?'

She hesitated, then her lips twisted into a wry smile. 'Have you come home to make your peace with him, Sol?'

'Or?'

'Or to gloat?'

He leapt to his feet. 'You think I've—'

She held a finger to her lips and hitched her

head in the direction of the door. 'Mind the kitten.' It scampered between his feet and settled under his chair. Another one joined it. Gingerly he lowered himself back to his seat, but he couldn't unbend his backbone.

'Look, Sol, I do understand.'

He wished to hell *he* did.

'I had a mother like Alec, remember?'

Yeah, he remembered. Some days he wished to hell he could forget. 'And you always called her Mum. Did you make your peace with *her* before she died?'

A curtain of hair fell across her face, hiding her eyes, and he immediately regretted his harshness. He shouldn't take this out on her. She was the last person who deserved it.

'No, I never made peace with my mother. She never stopped drinking long enough for me to try it.'

Hell, she wasn't going to cry, was she? Cassie never cried. He hadn't—

'And now she's dead.' She smiled at him. A sad little smile that speared right through the centre of him.

He reached out and covered her hand with his. 'You didn't deserve that, Cassie.'

She turned her hand over and squeezed. 'Neither did you.'

A great hole opened up inside him when she tugged her hand free.

'I hear you're a hotshot architect these days.'

She didn't want to talk about the past. She'd moved on. He set his shoulders. So had he.

'Have you come home to build me that tree house?'

Her words startled a laugh as memory flashed through him. 'I'd forgotten all about that.'

'I hadn't.'

Something in her tone had his eyes swinging back to hers. She had the most amazing eyes— violet, with the deep, soft texture of velvet. He had a feeling she remembered everything. He shied away from the thought. 'I even drew up plans for that tree house.' How could he have forgotten? He'd slaved over those drawings for weeks.

'I remember those too.' Her laughter engulfed him in warmth. 'We couldn't find a tree big enough to house it.'

'I aimed high.'

'And you succeeded.'

Her words were soft and spoken with real pleasure. It made him ashamed of avoiding…

He drew in a deep breath. 'I heard about Brian. I'm real sorry, Cassie.'

That curtain of hair fell across her face, hiding it. Her hands trembled and a shaft of pain shot straight through him.

Cassie's insides knotted and twisted. Her face tightened. None of the platitudes she normally mumbled rose to her lips or to her rescue. She tried desperately to untwist, unknot, unwind herself.

Idiot. Did you really think you could get through an entire conversation without Brian being mentioned?

She flicked her hair back, recognised the concern in Sol's eyes and hated it. For a moment she was tempted to let her hair fall back to hide her eyes, to help her lie, but she couldn't lie— not to Sol. He'd know.

'Last Christmas was hell.' That at least was the truth. She twisted her wedding band round and round her finger. 'So, I'm making doubly sure this Christmas isn't.'

Gratitude surged through her when with one curt nod he let the subject drop. She cleared her throat.

'What are your plans? Are you staying for Christmas?'

'Yep.'

Delight tiptoed through her. 'But that's fabulous.' Christmas was only nine days away. She risked a glance at his face but she couldn't read it. It brought her up short for a moment, then she shrugged. Ten years was a long time. 'What will you do on Christmas Day?'

He raised an eyebrow, took one look at her face, then grimaced. 'Sorry to burst your bubble and all, but Christmas is just like any other day as far as I'm concerned.'

'Is that so?' She folded her arms.

He shifted in his seat. 'Look, I—'

'It used to mean a lot when we were kids and we didn't get a Christmas.'

'Is that why you have to have a Christmas now?' he shot at her.

'Is that why you don't?' she shot back, just as quickly.

They stared at each other for a moment, then laughed. But she settled on one thing then and there. Sol was having a Christmas this year whether he said he wanted it or not. Everyone needed a Christmas.

And Sol hadn't had one since he was twelve.

She glanced across at him. Man, oh, man, it was good to have him home. She drank in the sight of him while he stared out at the yard with that shuttered half-gaze she remembered so well. Sol had always been a good-looking boy. But that was what he'd been when he'd left. He had certainly changed since then. He had grown up now.

He was a man. And what a man.

A pulse started to throb at the base of her throat. He was every kind of hunk she could think of and then some. He was going to set the female population of Schofield on its collective head.

His eyes hadn't changed, though. Still black, still piercing, still kind. And given half a chance they could probably still see right through her. She lifted the kitten clambering up her leg into her lap. She couldn't give Sol that chance—not even a quarter of that chance. The kitten settled into her lap, purring.

She glanced around the Adams' back veranda. It and the attached laundry ran the length of the house. She sprang to her feet and walked its length, glancing right and left then swung back, clutching the kitten to her chest. 'Sol, I need a favour.'

'Anything.'

A shockwave rippled through her at the promptness of his reply, at its certainty. 'Is that wise?' she demanded. He chuckled, and the sound of it washed over the surface of her skin with the velvet warmth of hot chocolate. She wanted to stretch and purr beneath it.

'I may not have clapped eyes on you for ten years, Cassie Campbell…Parker, but I still know you.'

'I might have changed.'

He paused. His eyes raked over her and darkened. 'You have at that.'

Cassie fell back into her chair. She crossed her

right leg over her left. Her foot bounced and wouldn't stop. She set it on the floor, but that set her knees jiggling. She crossed her legs again and let the foot bounce.

'Lookin' good, Cassie.'

Her foot stopped mid-bounce. His eyes roved over her face, and her skin flushed everywhere his gaze touched.

'Real good.'

'Thank you,' she croaked. She seized her glass. 'You're not looking too bad yourself.' But she didn't look at him as she said it. She took swallow after swallow of cold water, but it didn't cool the heat rising through her.

'What's this favour?'

The favour. Right. She set her glass down. 'Would you babysit my kittens?'

'Babysit?'

'Until Christmas?'

'Christmas!'

'I can't take them home because Rufus will eat them. I've kept them locked up in the laundry of the old place—' she nodded across the yard '—while it's between tenants, but it's so tiny, and it's mean keeping them there for such long periods. They won't be any trouble, I swear.'

He looked sceptical, and she didn't blame him. 'You don't need to do anything. I'll come over every evening to feed them.'

'You will?'

'Then I'll lock them up in your laundry for the night.'

'You'll come over every evening?'

'Every evening,' she assured him. 'So all you need to do is let them out of the laundry each morning. That's it.'

'That's it, huh?'

'That's it.' She shrugged, then slanted him a grin. 'Though even if you say no I'll still be here each evening. I'm Alec's home-care help.'

'Home-care help?'

'It's a community-based programme designed to help people stay in their own homes longer by helping them out with housework, meals and stuff.'

'You do that?'

She shrugged, abashed by the warmth in his voice. 'I love it.'

'How long have you been doing it?'

Her eyes slid from his. 'Ten years.'

There was a long silence. Finally Sol asked, 'How long have you been helping Alec?'

'Two years.'

'Two years?' He jerked around to face her fully. 'He's been sick for two years and he never told me?'

'He's being looked after.'

'Yeah, but—'

'But what? You'd have come home, seen he was getting the right kind of care, then left again.'

He raked a hand through his hair. 'How long has he got?'

'You're a better man than I if you can get a straight answer to that one,' she sighed.

He stared back out at the yard and Cassie's chest ached. Why did it have to be such hell sometimes? Who had decided Sol should draw the short straw where family was concerned—the shortest of short straws—when Brian had had so much?

She froze that thought. Brian was dead. He didn't have anything any more.

'Why didn't you let me know, Cassie? You could've rung or written.'

'It was Alec's choice. His decision to make.' Her hands twisted together in her lap.

'And?'

His eyes didn't leave her face. It was almost frightening the way he could still read her. 'And you didn't answer the last time I wrote to you.'

His eyes darkened, then shuttered, and something inside Cassie squeezed painfully.

'I would've come back for this.'

But her wedding hadn't been important enough? It was as if he'd wiped Schofield from his mind completely. And her with it. 'You left this town and all of us in it far behind.' And maybe it had been for the best. 'I never thought you'd come back. Ever. I didn't try and get in touch with you because I thought hearing from me, hearing from anyone in Schofield, would be just about the last thing you'd want.'

His hands clenched into fists as he turned and stared at her. 'Then you were wrong.'

'You could've let me know that ten years ago.'

He stared back out at the yard and Cassie

shivered. She'd never seen his eyes so dark…so…

Her mouth went dry. 'Why have you come back, Sol?'

He shrugged. 'Curiosity, I guess.'

He met her eyes, but the darkness still lurked in them and Cassie knew he was lying. She just didn't know why.

CHAPTER TWO

'It's pretty hot, Alec. Are you sure you wouldn't prefer a salad?'

'Sausages, mash, peas and carrots,' Alec repeated. 'I don't care how hot it is.'

'Okay, okay.' She pulled the sausages out of the fridge. 'Catch.' She tossed him a carrot. 'Peel that while I take care of the potatoes.' She smothered a grin at his grumbling. She knew he liked her being here, bossing him about, not treating him like an invalid. 'Where's Sol?'

'Out.'

'Out?' she parroted stupidly, then bit her lip to stop herself from asking, *Out where?*

'Why'd you have to go and rile him up earlier?'

Indignation slugged through her. 'I did no such thing.'

'Humph.'

Or had she? She popped the sausages under the grill. 'Maybe being home has riled him.'

'Humph.'

'You have to admit he can't have many fond memories of living here.'

Alec didn't even humph this time. He stayed silent.

'Do you like having him back?' She probably shouldn't have asked but she couldn't help it. Alec had not been a kind father. In fact, at times he'd been downright mean. That was what alcohol had done to him. But, as she'd told Sol earlier, Alec hadn't had a drink in over two years. He'd changed. He'd mellowed. And she sensed he regretted the past.

She sliced the carrot. It didn't mean he was glad to see Sol, though. Maybe he resented the reminder of a past that filled him with shame?

'It's good to see the lad,' Alec mumbled.

She tried to school her surprise. 'Good.' His words made her fiercely glad and fiercely angry all at the same time. 'Have you told him so?'

'Humph.'

She turned the sausages. 'I think you should tell him.' She met his eyes. 'Don't you let him leave like he did last time.' That would be too awful for words.

The older man's eyes dropped. 'He hasn't come back to see me.'

She had an uncanny feeling Alec was right. 'Maybe not,' she agreed. 'But all the same—'

'Go on, tell me I deserve it.'

'Okay, you deserve it.' A shaft of pity spiked through her as he hunched in his wheelchair. 'But you've an opportunity with him now that you never thought you'd get again. Make the most of it.'

He glanced at her. 'You think there's a chance?'

'There's always a chance.' She set a place for him at the table. 'Just don't let him leave like he did last time.'

Maybe Alec didn't deserve a second chance with Sol, but she knew if her mother had given her one she'd have jumped at it.

Maybe Sol was different. Maybe he—

No. She and Sol were two of a kind. Or they

always had been, and ten years couldn't change him that much.

She dropped into the seat opposite. 'Tell me, Alec, do you have a Christmas tree?'

Cassie bounded up the back steps and into the kitchen. 'Sorry I'm late, Jean.' She kissed the older woman's cheek.

'You're not late. You're right on time.'

Cassie took in the tired lines around Jean's eyes and a shaft of guilt speared through her. Normally she arrived early on a Thursday night to help prepare the meal. 'What can I do?'

'It's all under control, dear.' Jean picked up a platter of fried chicken. 'You could bring those salads through.'

Cassie seized the bowls and followed Jean into the dining room to find the rest of the family already assembled. With a smile she relaxed into them. The Parkers—the family Brian had given her. And Thursday night was family night, when they all gathered here at Jack and Jean's.

She loved them with a fierceness born of desperation. The desperation of someone who'd never had a family or known family life until they'd hugged her to their collective bosom with a warmth that had taken her breath away.

It still did, really.

She slipped into her seat beside Tracey, Brian's younger sister, and across from Fran, his older one. Fran's husband Claude beamed with good health and good cheer beside Fran. Cassie figured he had a lot to be cheerful about. She averted her eyes from the bulge burgeoning under Fran's dress, tried to dispel the ache that gripped her.

From the corner of her eye she watched Jack as he said grace. He looked tired too. Neither he nor Jean had slept well since Brian's death. Cassie smothered a sigh. It had been nearly eighteen months. She'd hoped...

Hoped what? Brian had been their golden boy—the whole town's golden boy. The rugby genius who'd played for Australia and put the town of Schofield on the map. Some things you just didn't get over, ever. And for Jean and Jack she had a feeling Brian's death was one of them.

Maybe if she'd produced that much-wanted

grandchild… She smothered another sigh and thrust the thought away, averting her eyes from Fran's tummy as best she could.

'How is your work going, Cassandra?'

She shot Jack a smile. 'Fabulous.' She knew how proud they all were of her community work. But then, they were a community-minded family. It was one of the reasons the town had rallied around so much when Brian had died. 'Maisie's twin nieces showed up the day before yesterday.'

'Ooh, how are they?' Jean cut in, always interested to hear news of youngsters who no longer lived in Schofield.

'Great. You'll never guess what they've done.' She handed the potato salad across to Claude. 'They've packed her a suitcase and whisked her off on a cruise for Christmas.'

'How lovely.' Jean clasped her hands together. 'They always were nice girls, and so was their mother. It was a real tragedy, her dying so young.'

Silence enveloped them. As it always did when death was mentioned. She could almost see the image of Brian sweep across the table.

Tracey cleared her throat. 'You and Dad should go on a cruise, Mum.'

'Oh, no, dear, we couldn't.'

'Why not?' Tracey persisted.

'Well, now… I mean…'

'Your mother means our life is here.'

Cassie gulped as Jack glared at his youngest daughter. 'Guess who I saw today?' she jumped in, before Tracey could argue her point further. 'You'll never guess, so I'll have to tell you.' She accepted a bread roll from the basket Jean held out to her. She smiled around the table. 'Sol Adams.'

Tracey and Jack stopped glaring at each other to gape at her. Jean dropped the basket of bread rolls.

'Sol Adams?' Fran frowned, as if trying to place him.

'Yes—you remember,' Tracey leaned forward, excitement shooting from her in all directions. 'He was in Cassie and Brian's year. Seriously hunky.' She turned to Cassie. 'Have you actually seen him?'

'Sure.' She helped Jean pick up the scattered bread rolls. 'He's staying with Alec.'

'Omigod, all the girls in my year had serious crushes on him.'

Cassie's eyebrows shot up towards her hairline. 'Really?'

Tracey rolled her eyes. 'All the girls in your year just couldn't see past Brian, but we knew better.'

'Tracey Phyllis Parker!' Jean looked as if she were about to cry. 'How on earth can you say such a thing? And with Cassie sitting here and all.'

Tracey glanced at Cassie, stricken. 'I'm sorry, Cassie. I didn't—'

'Relax, Mum. Cassie's fine—aren't you?' Fran's even tones broke over them and Cassie nodded gratefully. 'No sister is going to find her brother a hunk. Not even the sisters of the legendary Brian Parker.'

'Yes, well, I suppose you're right,' Jean sighed. 'But even so.'

'Even so what?' Fran teased.

'Even so, we know that Sol Adams isn't half the man Brian was. Isn't that so, Cassandra?'

A band tightened around Cassie's chest, trying to suffocate her.

'Nonsense,' Tracey scoffed.

'Isn't that so, Cassandra?' Jack persisted.

Cassie forced a smile. 'I married Brian, so that makes me biased.' Though maybe not in the way Jack thought. 'Sol didn't have things easy.' Not like Brian. The words hung in the air unsaid. She bit her lip. 'He was always nice to me. We were neighbours.' She shrugged. 'We were friends.' She could tell Jack didn't like her words.

'So what did he have to say? What did you talk about? Has he changed?'

Tracey's gunfire questions made Cassie laugh. 'It's been ten years. Sure he's changed. We all have.'

'You've got prettier.' Tracey said the words as a statement of fact. 'Is Sol hunkier?'

Is he *what?* But she couldn't tell them that! 'I, uh, I don't know.' Jack shot Tracey a triumphant glare, and Cassie couldn't help herself. 'He's filled out…grown into all that height. Remember how he used to be kind of gangly and lanky?' Tracey nodded eagerly. 'Well, he's not any more.'

Jack concentrated on the plate of food in front of him and Jean's gaze darted from Cassie to

Tracey and back again. Remorse stabbed her. She shouldn't have said anything.

'What did you talk about?'

She wished to heaven she hadn't mentioned Sol Adams now. She seized another drumstick, even though she hadn't touched her first. 'We chatted about Alec, mostly.'

'And?'

And his hand on mine felt fabulous. But she had no intention of telling anyone that either. 'And…' She floundered for a moment. 'And he's babysitting my kittens.'

'He is?' Tracey blinked. 'Sol is a cat person?'

That made Cassie grin. 'No, I don't think he is. He looked as if he'd sucked a lemon when I asked him.' She could tell he wasn't a cat person, but he'd still said yes. The thought warmed her.

Jack smirked. 'I can't say I blame him.'

Jack wasn't a cat person. He wasn't really a dog person either. He was a hunting and fishing kind of person.

Jean leaned across the table. 'We should've let Cassie keep those kittens here.'

'Nonsense,' he chuckled, suddenly smug. 'Sol Adams can look after them. It serves him right.'

For what? Why didn't Jack like Sol? She bit back a sigh. Maybe it was another reminder that a person from his son's generation was alive when his son was not.

'Can you set me up with him?' Tracey suddenly demanded.

Cassie choked on fried chicken. 'What?'

'Could you arrange a blind date for us or… better yet…have a dinner to welcome him back to town?'

Gee, she could just see Sol jumping at that.

'How about Saturday night?'

No! It was a terrible idea. It was—

'For Pete's sake, Tracey, leave Cassandra in peace.' Jack's smugness had fled. His jaw clenched and his eyes flashed fire. 'Let her finish her dinner.'

Tracey subsided, but Cassie could tell by the stubborn light in her eyes that it was only a momentary reprieve. As soon as Tracey got her alone she'd renew her appeal. Cassie glanced around the table and her heart sank.

Since when had she been able to deny any member of this family anything?

Sol knocked, then shifted from one foot to the other. He glanced down at his watch. Hell. It was still early. He hoped Cassie was up.

One thing. She'd asked him to do one thing and he couldn't even manage that. He'd been a fool to come back.

He knocked again. Under his breath he started to count. 'One, two…' He'd knock again when he got to ten. 'Three, four…' Would she go ballistic? Every other woman he knew would throw a hissy fit. 'Five, six…' A reluctant grin tugged at the corners of his mouth. He couldn't see Cassie throwing a hissy fit. 'Seven, eight…' The grin disappeared. She loved those kittens. She'd told him so. 'Nine—'

The door cracked open a fraction. One velvet eye peered through the gap, then the door flew open. 'Sol! What are you doing here?'

He stared at her, and for the life of him he couldn't remember. The thin terry-towelling robe she wore would've been more than respectable in ordinary circumstances, but not now—not when she was so wet. He must've hauled her out of the shower. He gulped. Her wet hair dripped down the front of the robe, outlining a shape that had his tongue fastening to the roof of his mouth. He dragged in a breath. Keep breathing, Adams. You can do it. It's easy.

No, it wasn't. It was damn hard. Cassie's curves were as lush and gorgeous as the woman herself. Need pierced through him. His knees almost buckled. He wanted to haul her into his arms and—

He tried to extinguish the pictures that rose in his mind. He could see Cassie's lips moving, but no sound reached his ears. He rubbed a hand over his face.

'Sol?' Her forehead creased in concern. 'Are you okay?'

He was a lot of things, but okay wasn't one of them. And he had no intention of telling her that. 'I, er, didn't sleep too well last night.' At least that was the truth.

'What are you doing here?'

Aw, hell—that's right. The kittens. Remember? Ballistic hissy fits and stuff? Ballistic he could cope with. He eyed her warily. As long as she didn't cry. 'I, er…' He scuffed the toe of his sneaker against the top step.

'Yes?' She drew the word out as if tempted to shake him.

'I seem to have lost one of your kittens.'

'Oh, I'm sorry, Sol.'

She was sorry? She was sorry!

'You'd better come in.' She grabbed his arm and pulled him inside. She tossed a quick glance outside before she slammed the door, then led him into the living room.

He looked around and his jaw dropped.

'I lied to you, you know?'

He forced himself to focus on her words, her face, rather than the surroundings. If he didn't he'd explode. Or implode. Or he'd fall into an abyss he'd never get out of again. 'Lied?' He latched onto the word.

'I told you the kittens wouldn't be any trouble.'

She started to dry her hair vigorously, as if suddenly aware of how it dripped down the front of her robe. The action made bits of her jiggle.

Bits he shouldn't be staring at if he didn't want himself called a male chauvinist pig.

He stared at the wall behind her. An enormous photo of Brian holding up a trophy and surrounded by his Australian team-mates dominated the space. His gut clenched at the triumphant grin on Brian's face. He glanced to his left. An enormous trophy cabinet stood there. He swung away to his right and another wall of photographs rose out at him—Brian scoring the winning try in some grand final, Brian awarded the sportsman's medal of the year, Brian on the shoulders of his team-mates.

Brian. Brian. Brian.

'What is this?' he suddenly burst out. 'A mausoleum?'

He immediately wished he'd kept his fat trap shut when Cassie stepped back from him, her eyes dark.

'I'm sorry.' He took a step towards her and she took another step back. He stayed put and held up his hands. 'I'm sorry. I shouldn't have said anything.'

'I, uh, the kitchen is through there if you want

to grab a coffee. I'll go get dressed.' And then she was gone.

Sol tossed another glance around, then left the room with a grimace. His gut clenched again when he entered the kitchen. Evidence Cassie had shared this house with Brian was everywhere. His eyes rested on a coffee mug on the sideboard. It read: 'Old rugby players never die they just…' He didn't have the heart to turn it over and read the punchline. Brian had been a rugby player, a good one, but he hadn't been old. And he shouldn't be dead.

He pushed through the back door, needing air. An enormous dog lifted his head from a kennel, his ears pricked forward. Sol sat on the lowest step, rested his elbows on his knees and stared back. 'Are you Cassie's dog or Brian's?'

The dog sat up, stretched and shook his head.

'Fair enough,' Sol said, and patted his knee. The dog trotted over. Sol scratched his ears then reached for the tag around the dog's neck. 'Rufus.' The dog's tail thumped harder. 'Ah, the eater of kittens. Well, Rufus, were you sad when Brian died?' The tail kept thumping. 'I wasn't.

Not really.' He hadn't been happy either, but it hadn't been till now that the tragedy had hit him—that someone as young as Brian, as full of life as Brian, was dead.

He'd been sad for Cassie, but he hadn't thought about the living hell she must've gone through. Could still be going through. He dragged a hand down his face. She was too young to be a grieving widow. And he hadn't offered her any kind of condolence, any kind of comfort. His lips twisted. He knew Cassie. She'd have put on a brave face for the rest of the world and then grieved alone. He could've helped.

But he hadn't. And if the truth be known his first emotion when he'd heard about Brian's death had been one of hope. He shook his head. It could never be that simple, though, could it? He'd always resented Brian. Resented how easy he'd had it. Resented his offhand attitude to everything he had.

And then there'd been Cassie.

A gasp sounded behind him and he spun around. He met Cassie's eyes through the screen door. They were wide and frightened. A hand fluttered to her mouth.

He leapt to his feet. 'What's wrong?' What had scared her?

She drew in a shaky breath. 'Upon my word, you like to take your life in your own hands, don't you, Sol Adams?'

'What are you talking about?'

'Rufus here likes to eat strangers for breakfast.'

A smile stretched across his face. He didn't deserve it, he acknowledged that much, but Cassie cared. She didn't want him torn limb from limb by a dog.

It doesn't mean anything, a voice in his head said. Cassie wouldn't want anyone torn limb from limb.

It's a start, his stubborn heart returned. 'Me and Rufus here—' Rufus wagged his tail '—have come to an understanding.'

Cassie folded her arms. 'Really?'

'I scratch his belly and he doesn't eat me. He's a big pussycat.'

'Correction. He eats pussycats. And speaking of cats…'

She was right. 'Let's go.' He hoped to hell they could find the kitten. He didn't want to let her down. 'I'm sorry I didn't keep a closer eye on them for you.'

'It's not your fault.' She locked the front door. 'They're the Houdini quartet. I bet it's Rudolph who's missing.'

'Rudolph?'

'The little one.'

He opened the car door for her. 'Yep.'

'Do you know how long he's been gone?'

'He wasn't with the others when I let them out of the laundry.' She bit her lip and fresh wave of guilt engulfed him. The kitten could've been out all night.

'You checked inside the washing machine?'

'Yep.' He'd turned the entire laundry upside down. 'There's a spot under the washing machine where the floorboards have perished. My guess is he wriggled out of there somehow. I mean, it's only the smallest of gaps—'

'Rudolph only needs the smallest of gaps.' She sighed. 'We're lucky the others didn't follow.'

'Well, they won't now. I've boarded it up.'

A shadow fell across the car. 'Is everything okay, Cass?'

Cassie swung around. 'Keith!' She beamed at the other man and something dark and ugly slugged through Sol's gut. She gestured to Sol. 'Do you remember Sol Adams?'

Sol sure as hell remembered Keith Sinclair, Brian's best mate. Keith nodded, but didn't offer his hand. Sol nodded back. He didn't offer his hand either.

'Is everything okay?' Keith repeated.

'Sure it is.' Cassie's smile widened. 'I talked Sol here into letting me use his back veranda for my kittens, but one of them has got out.'

'Again?'

Again? Sol felt a little better. If these kittens had priors for escaping…

'But they're presents for your oldies.'

Sol didn't know whether to laugh or not at the look on Keith's face.

'I'm sure we'll find it,' Cassie soothed, but Keith had already hauled his mobile phone out of his pocket.

'We'll help.'

'Really, Keith, it's not necessary. You'll be late for work.'

'Not a problem, Cass. You know we're here for you.'

'But I—'

'And we know how important those kittens are to you.'

It took Keith less than ten minutes to have a search party organised. A search party that consisted of Brian's old mates—all members of the Rugby League Club. Sol didn't know what to say, and he sure didn't know what to think. Were they all in love with Cassie? Was this some kind of weird collective courting ritual? The dark glares they tossed him had his mind working overtime.

He turned to Cassie and she shrugged an apology. But her eyes danced, as if she wanted to burst out laughing. He glanced around again and had to clamp down on that same impulse. Six grown men crawled around Alec's backyard calling, 'Kitty, kitty. Here, kitty, kitty.' Any of these men would rather be dead than seen cradling a tiny kitten in their arms, yet here they were—

'What on earth is all this racket?'

Alec burst out onto the back veranda still in his

pyjamas, a scowl on his face and a kitten in his lap. Sol and Cassie stared at each other, then Cassie covered a grin with her hand. 'Didn't check the house, huh, Sol?'

'How did it get inside? There's no way—'

'The damn thing was mewling out the front in the middle of the night,' Alec grumbled.

Cassie smiled. 'So you went out and got him?'

What Sol wouldn't do to have her smile at him like that.

'I had to,' Alec grouched. 'In the interests of peace and quiet and sleep.'

Sol noticed he didn't offer to hand the kitten back.

'The search is over, boys,' Cassie called out.

'You want a lift home, Cass?'

'No, thanks, Keith. I promised to help Alec out with something this morning.'

She had?

'You'll make sure she gets home safe, Adams?'

'Nah,' some devil made him say, 'she can catch a cab.' All the men bristled, and he saw Cassie try to hide another grin. 'Of course I'll see her home.'

Muttering, the men left. As the last car drove

away, Sol turned to her, arms upraised. 'What was that all about?'

'You didn't get it?' She stared at him expectantly. 'C'mon, Sol. All those guys idolised Brian, right?'

He shrugged. 'I guess.'

'And I'm Brian's widow.' She enunciated each word with deliberate care.

'Uh-huh.' He could've done without that reminder.

She gave an exaggerated sigh. 'You still don't get it? Brian put Schofield on the map and the town adored him for it. As his widow, they adore me too.'

So they should. But for who she was, not because she'd married Brian Parker. Her fragrance curled around him as he followed her into the house. She smelt like Christmas—a cross between pinecones and plum pudding.

'You have no idea how fabulous this widowhood caper is.'

His jaw dropped. 'Fabulous?'

'You bet. I have a whole town that'll do anything for me. You just saw.'

He sure had.

'I'm surrounded by people eager to help me out.' She filled the kettle, then leant a hip against the kitchen sink. 'If I don't get a chance to walk Rufus, Max next door does it for me. Keith and Phillip take it in turns to mow my lawn. If I need an odd job done around the house it's done—' she snapped her fingers '—like that. Every home gardener in the neighbourhood supplies me with more fruit and veggies than I know what to do with. And eggs—I get lots of eggs.' She grinned. 'Everyone looks out for me.'

Unease slugged through him. 'And you like that?' It'd suffocate the hell out of him.

'I love it, and what's more…' she sent him a mischievous grin '…I don't have the mean girls at school saying, "Poor Cassie; she still hasn't found herself a man," and I get it all without the bother of having a husband.'

He gripped the back of the chair. 'Was Brian a bother?'

The curtain of hair immediately hid her face.

* * *

Damn, damn and double damn. What had made her go and rattle on like that?

'Cassie?'

'From what I hear all husbands are a bother.' She tried for light. It didn't work. Or at least Sol didn't buy it. Panic scurried through her. 'Brian is dead.' She couldn't hide the pain that stretched across her voice. She just hoped to God she'd managed to hide the guilt.

'So, if you can't have Brian this is the next best thing?'

No. God forgive her. Being Brian's widow was the best thing. But she couldn't tell Sol that. She couldn't tell anyone.

He sat heavily when she remained silent. 'I see.'

She doubted that. And she was glad, she told herself fiercely. She didn't want anyone to see. She lifted her chin. 'I'm never, *ever* getting married again.'

'Don't say that, Cassie.' He reached across and took her hand. 'I swear you can find what you had with Brian again.'

Exactly. That was what she was afraid of.

'And give up all this?'

Alec wheeled back into the kitchen and she tugged her hand free, tried to slow the stupid scampering of her heart. Alec had changed out of his pyjamas, but he still had the kitten on his lap. Maybe she'd misjudged him? Maybe he'd like a kitten to love?

She glanced at her watch. 'I'm afraid I have to get going.' She should've taken the ride Keith had offered. But Sol had smelt too good, looked too good, for her to surrender all hopes of sharing at least one cup of coffee with him this morning.

Bad idea. Look where that temptation had landed her. *Idiot.* She was not risking everything she'd built up here in Schofield because some man smelt good and looked good.

Sol surveyed her for a long moment. 'I thought you had to help Alec out with something.'

Alec glanced up. 'You do?'

'Sure I do. But it'll have to wait till this afternoon.'

'You just put the kettle on,' Sol pointed out.

'I…umm…habit. I don't have time now.' She headed for the front door and tried not to breathe too deeply as she walked past him.

CHAPTER THREE

'HELLO?' Cassie called through the back door as kittens clambered over her feet. 'Anyone home?'

The day before yesterday she'd have waltzed straight in, calling for Alec, but not today. Not when Sol was living here. What if he were one of those people who walked around their house naked?

After all, it was hot.

Heat that had nothing to do with summer temperatures surged through her. She really didn't want to walk in on a naked Sol. She fanned a hand in front of her face, trying to cool down. She really didn't. Honest. Though half naked would be nice. She wouldn't mind seeing him without his shirt, just to see how much he'd changed in ten years. Just to see if his shoulders promised—

Arghh. Can that thought right now, Cassie Parker. You don't fantasise about near-naked men.

'Wrong. I quite obviously do,' she muttered, wondering at the political correctness of such an admission.

'Do what?'

Sol loomed on the other side of the screen door, and for a moment all Cassie could do was stare. 'Uh, make a sterling scratching post,' she gulped. She bent down to detach a kitten from her leg. When she straightened, she prayed her face wasn't red.

Alec wheeled up behind Sol. 'You're early again,' he grumbled.

'Yes, I am.' Alec still had the kitten on his lap. It curled up there as if it never meant to leave. 'Well, aren't you going to let me in?' she demanded, as both men stared at her. Sol shook himself, then pushed the door open. 'Have I got something on my face?' She scrubbed a hand across her face as both men continued to stare. Sol sent her a lop-sided grin that had her stomach falling all over itself.

He pointed. 'On your head.'

'My Santa hat?' She twirled on the spot. 'Do you like it? I wore it specially.'

'Humph.' Alec backed up and wheeled away.

'It looks hot,' Sol said.

Her eyes narrowed. Man, did this place need some Christmas cheer or what? She followed him into the kitchen. 'It certainly captures the spirit of the afternoon.'

Both men swung around to stare at her suspiciously. She beamed back at them. 'We're putting up your Christmas tree.' She held up one hand as they both opened their mouths to argue. 'I have my heart set on decorating your Christmas tree, and don't forget that I'm the town's favourite widow and only blackguards without scruple would disappoint me.

'Furthermore,' she added when they both opened their mouths again, 'if you don't play along, you—' she glared at Alec '—will get nothing but salad for tea tonight. And you—' she glared at Sol '—won't get invited to my place for dinner tomorrow night.' Both men chewed her words over for a moment, then subsided into silence. 'Fabulous.' She dusted off her hands. 'Okay—Alec, you organise the drinks and you, Sol, can drag the Christmas tree out of the hall closet.'

She walked through to the living room and chose her spot—smack-bang in the middle of the front window, so everyone who drove by could see it. Not that many people drove out this way.

The curtains fluttered in the breeze. She lifted her face to it. Sol's doing, she'd bet. For the life of her she didn't know why Alec kept everything so shut up.

Yes, she did. Alec kept his house shut up the way he kept himself shut up. It was a simple as that.

And as complicated.

'Where do you want me to dump this?'

Sol stood in the doorway, a large box in his arms, and a strange pulse fluttered to life in her throat. His arm muscles bulged as if he was used to manual labour. She gulped. Ten years ago—

He shifted the box. 'Have I got something on *my* face?'

She blinked, then made herself grin. Pushing

the coffee table to one side, she pointed. 'I'd like you to *place* the box there.' He chuckled at her stress on the word, and, oh, heavens, there it was again, that warm hot chocolate glow. He glanced at her strangely, so she shook herself and said, 'Show me your hands.'

He immediately held them out, palm upward, like a little boy proving he'd washed his hands before dinner. She took one of them between her own and traced the calluses with her fingers. His hands matched his arms. Big and masculine. The kind of hands a woman could imagine holding her. Tracing and caressing and—

She dropped the hand and shoved hers behind her back. 'I thought you were an architect.' The words rapped out of her like bullets. 'I mean, I thought you designed houses, not built them.'

'I do.'

His eyes settled on her, and awareness shot up her backbone.

'But I like to get involved in all stages of my projects. I've even built my own house.'

'From scratch?'

'Yep.'

'All on your own?'

He shrugged. 'I had plumbers in to do the plumbing and electricians in to wire the house.'

'But the rest you did all on your own?' Her mouth opened and closed. 'But that's amazing.' She couldn't imagine Brian—

'Nah, it's not.'

But he looked pleased all the same, and as their eyes met that awareness arced between them again. Cassie found her palms suddenly damp. It was the heat, she told herself. Summer day heat. She wiped her palms down the front of her skirt. 'Then this—' she pointed to the box '—should be a cinch for you.'

Alec wheeled into the room with both tray and kitten perched precariously on his knee. Cassie's jaw dropped. 'What do you think you're doing?' She pointed to the tray. It held two cans of beer, a jug of homemade lemonade and three glasses. Wasn't it only yesterday she'd bragged to Sol that Alec hadn't had a drink in two years? And yet here—

'Keep your hat on.' He scowled. 'The beers are for you and Sol. The boy can't be expected to live on my lolly water, now, can he?'

'I suppose not.' Though Alec's lemonade was delicious.

'And I thought, seeing as you're all set on this Christmas spirit thing, that you'd join the boy in a drink.'

'A beer?'

'Anything wrong with that?' Sol asked.

'No.' She drew the word out slowly. It was just that nobody ever offered her beer. Ever. Wine and soft drinks, yes, but not beer.

Her lips twisted. Brian could still exert his influence, even from the grave. He hadn't liked her drinking beer—hadn't thought it was ladylike. So she hadn't drunk it. Just like that. It was crazy to give up your freedom so easily, but she had. Without so much as a whimper. And now she lived in a town that thought she didn't like beer.

'Cassie?'

She lifted her chin. 'I'd love a beer.' She seized one and popped the top. Further, she was going to drink it straight from the can. Sol and Alec wouldn't mind. Heck, they probably wouldn't even notice.

'Cheers.' She raised the can in salute, then took a long swig, savouring its strong flavour. She wiped her mouth with the back of her hand and beamed at the two men.

Sol grinned, as if her enthusiasm amused him. 'Good?'

'The best,' she vowed. 'Now, chop-chop. Haul that thing out of its box.'

'Heavens, Alec,' she breathed later, as she and Sol set about erecting the tree. 'How tall is this thing?'

'Nearly seven feet.' An idle hand stroked the kitten.

He didn't strike Cassie as the kind of man who went in for Christmas trees—especially not enormous seven-foot monstrosities. But then she hadn't thought he'd take to a kitten either.

'Sol's mum,' he said, as if he could read the question in her face. 'She got some freak in her head.'

'As was her wont,' she heard Sol mutter under his breath. She understood. Pearl Adams had been one erratic woman.

'She decided we had to have a Christmas tree, and of course, with Pearl, it had to be the biggest.' He took a slug of lemonade. 'It only got put up once.'

'Twice,' Sol corrected, then looked as if he wished he hadn't.

An awkward silence enveloped the room. Cassie looked from one man to the other, both with their closed and shuttered faces. She took another swig of beer and revelled for a moment in her newfound sense of freedom. 'Third time lucky, then. Isn't that what they say?'

Sol and Alec both looked charmingly non-plussed.

'Ooh, look—you've even got lights.' She pounced on them, then winked at Sol. 'We don't need a qualified electrician to wire up a tree. Come on—you start at the top. I won't reach. And here—' she handed Alec a box of red and green balls '—you start with these.'

Sol wound the lights around the top of the tree,

then handed them to her to arrange on the lower branches. She hummed *Deck the Halls,* and sensed rather than saw the two men roll their eyes at each other over her head.

'Why are you so into Christmas and all anyway, girl?' Alec grumbled as the kitten took a swipe at a Christmas ball.

'Maybe 'cos I never had a proper one when I was growing up.' She finished the lights and leaned back to survey their handiwork. Not bad. 'So I guess I'm making up for lost time.'

Alec stared at her for a moment and a shadow passed across his face. 'You trying to help an old reprobate like me make up for lost time too?'

Sol wouldn't mind knowing what she was up to himself.

'Ex-reprobate,' Cassie corrected.

She was right. Sol had to admit Alec had changed. A lot. And not just physically.

'That mama of yours, Cassie,' Alec shook his head. 'She shoulda…' He sighed. 'You was always a nice kid.'

'Yeah, I guess I was.' She hung red and green

balls on the branches Alec couldn't reach. 'So was Sol here.'

Silence greeted her words, then Alec chuckled. 'As a wee mite, if there was trouble to be found he'd be in the thick of it.'

She turned, hands on hips. 'He was a nice kid, Alec.'

Alec's gaze dropped. 'Yeah, Cassie. Sol here was a nice kid too. I'll grant you that.'

Sol couldn't believe his ears.

'He deserved to have Christmas too.'

'Yeah.' Alec shifted in his wheelchair. 'He did.'

'And he didn't deserve to have you beat up on him the way you used to.'

What did she think she was doing? 'Hell, Cassie,' he shot out the corner of his mouth, 'drop it. I thought we were going for Christmas spirit here. Just…'

'Just what?'

She raised an eyebrow. Somehow it only served to define the lush curve of her bottom lip. Sol swallowed. 'Just keep your nose out.'

Her eyes flashed fire. 'It's because people kept their noses out that I went hungry more often than

I should have. I made a promise to myself way back then, Sol Adams, to *never* keep my nose out.'

How did you argue with that?

'She's right, lad,' Alec mumbled, before shooting a glare at Cassie. 'You sure know how to make a man feel the lowest of the low, Cassie Campbell.'

'Parker,' she corrected.

Alec chuckled. 'You'll never be a Parker. They're good citizens and they mind their own business.'

'They're nice people, and you wouldn't feel ashamed of yourself if your conscience was clear,' she shot right back at him.

Sol laughed. He couldn't help it. 'Surrender now,' he advised Alec. 'You're never going to win against the likes of her.' He doubted anyone could. 'When did you go and get all bossy anyhow?' he asked her.

She tilted her nose and kept on decorating the tree. She tossed him some tinsel. 'Make yourself useful.'

'She's right, though, lad. I should never have whaled into you the way I did back then.'

Sol's jaw dropped. He half turned from twirling tinsel around the tree, then stopped. Discomfort crawled up his backbone and circled his skull. He didn't want to have this conversation. Not now, not ever.

'I'm sorry for what I did.'

Sol kept twining tinsel around the tree. Then ran out of tinsel.

'I don't expect you to forgive me. What I did back then—it wasn't right.'

Sol clenched his jaw. Started rearranging the tinsel.

'But I want you to know I regret it and…and I wish I could undo it or something.'

Sol's hands stilled. There was no mistaking the sincerity in Alec's voice. Silence crept into the room. He could feel Cassie's eyes on him, but he didn't know what response she wanted him to give. Even if he did he couldn't guarantee to give it.

She kicked his ankle. 'Oops, sorry.'

Eyebrows rose in mock innocence. Sympathy, laughter and gentleness all danced in the velvet violet of her eyes and somehow soothed him. He found himself smiling.

She smiled back. 'I think that was something important that needed to be said. Cheers.' She clinked both their drinks with her own.

Sol hesitated, then clinked his to Alec's. 'Cheers.'

'Cheers,' Alec returned gruffly, but his eyes were bright.

'Now, get out of your wheelchair for a moment, you decrepit old fogey. I need to stand on it to reach the top of the tree.'

Grumbling, Alec rose. Without thinking Sol offered him his arm. Alec accepted it. Carefully Cassie stood on the chair. Sol reached out to steady it. Stretching up, she placed a golden-haired angel on top of the tree.

Why did angels always have golden hair? Why not dark bobs that—

'Clap,' Cassie ordered. 'It's all done.'

Linking arms, Alec and Sol obeyed. It was a whole lot easier than arguing with her. Besides, she looked so pretty standing up there, her eyes bright, her cheeks flushed a real pretty pink, and Sol didn't have the heart to disappoint her. Or Alec. He had a feeling Alec was secretly enjoying this unexpected Christmas spirit as much as he.

No, not Christmas spirit. Cassie spirit.

He held out his hand to help her down and she clasped it lightly. If he hadn't had Alec propped up on his other arm he'd have swung her down by the waist for the sheer glory of feeling her in his arms. He had to content himself with her scent instead. It rushed at him, engulfing him, when she jumped down beside him.

He folded his thumb over her hand, keeping it within his own, not ready to let it go, and her eyes collided with his. Hunger stretched through him.

Her pupils dilated, the laughter on her lips died, then her gaze skittered away and, with a quick glance at Alec, she tugged her hand free.

Tomorrow night. Anticipation surged through him. She'd invited him round for dinner tomorrow night. And Alec wouldn't be there then. Maybe there was something to be said for being home for Christmas after all.

Sol pulled up at the front of Cassie's house, took in the three other cars lined up like a row of tin soldiers, and his gut clenched. Disappointment blazed a trail of acid down his throat to settle as a hard weight in the pit of his stomach.

This wasn't a cosy little dinner for two.

It was a dinner party. *Idiot!*

He switched off the ignition with a savage twist of his fingers. That's what you get when you don't ask questions—when you don't ask why you've been invited to dinner. His knuckles whitened where his hands clenched the steering wheel. He turned and glared at the bunch of daisies on the seat beside him. For a moment he was tempted to drive away, to leave and never come back.

He stared out through the windscreen, then unclenched his hands. Cassie didn't deserve that treatment from him. She hadn't ten years ago and she didn't now. Cassie had only ever wished him the best. She'd given her friendship freely, unstintingly. None of this was her fault. None of it.

And don't you forget it, Adams.

Still, it didn't stop his gut clenching when she

greeted him at the front door with that smile. She looked pretty in a hot pink skirt that fluttered around her knees and a lime-green halter-top. It showed off tanned shoulders and her exquisite shape without being overly sexy. He had a feeling Cassie avoided anything overly sexy.

She squeezed his hand. 'I'm glad you're here, Sol.'

The constriction around his chest loosened, then tightened again when, with a start, he saw she wore make-up. Not much, but enough to make her eyes big and smoky. Bigger and smokier, he amended. The peach shine on her lips made his mouth water.

She gazed back at him and the smoky eyes darkened and the peach lips parted and his stomach kicked. Then she drew back, tucked her hair behind her ears and brushed her left hand down across her skirt. Sol followed the action, saw the heavy gold band on her third finger and remembered the gulf that lay between them.

'Are they for me?' She nodded to the daisies, not meeting his eyes.

He unclenched his hand from around the stems

and prayed they'd stay together as he held them out to her.

'Thank you.' She buried her face in them. 'Now, come on through and meet the others.'

'The others' were Keith and Phillip, Brian's best mates from school, Phillip's wife, Geraldine and Brian's sister Tracey.

Brian. Brian. Brian.

Behind his eyes his head started to throb, but he eyed Tracey with frank curiosity. She raised a flirtatious eyebrow and sauntered over. Hell! She didn't still have a thing for him, did she?

'Do you remember Brian's sister, Tracey?' Cassie didn't meet his eye.

'Sure I do.'

'Daisies? Lucky you.' Tracey eyed them with frank appreciation. 'Did you know they were Cassie's favourites?'

Cassie stiffened.

'Are they?' Sol feigned surprise. 'I remember she used to grow them in her back garden. They were the only pretty things for miles around.'

Something flared in Tracey's eyes, then she blinked and it was gone. 'Roses are my favourites. The redder the better.'

The acid in his stomach eased. 'Roses, huh?' He grinned. He didn't know what she was up to, but she wasn't after him, thank God. 'Sounds like a hint.'

'Well, now, it's been a long time since anyone gave me flowers.' She twined one long blonde lock around her finger and slanted a glance at him through her lashes. 'And it is Christmas…so if you're offering…'

'I'll go put these in water,' Cassie blurted out, then hurried away.

Why the hell was Tracey flirting with him? He glanced around the room and found Keith glaring at Tracey. With a scowl, Keith turned and followed Cassie out of the room. 'Is there a thing between Cassie and Keith?'

Tracey snorted. 'You'd think so, the way he carries on, but no.' She grimaced up at him, all signs of flirtation gone. 'All of Brian's friends are protective of Cassie. Especially Keith.'

'I see.'

'Do you?' She folded her arms. 'This whole town has Cassie on a pedestal.'

The bitterness of her words rocked him. He swung back. 'I thought you and Cassie were friends.'

'We are.' Her eyes conveyed their shock, then they narrowed. 'Uh-huh—another one.'

He didn't like the way she surveyed him. 'Another what?'

She leaned in closer and stared at him hard. 'Why on earth would *you* put Cassie on a pedestal? You haven't even been around for the last ten years.'

Her words came a little too close to the sore spot in Sol's heart.

'She's a flesh-and-blood woman. How long is she going to be able to stay on that pedestal before toppling from it? And what'll happen to her when she does? This town didn't give her the time of day before she started dating Brian.'

'Why should—'

'She's being all things to everyone. How long can anyone keep that up?'

He opened his mouth, but Cassie came back

into the room and he couldn't help it. His eyes followed her. She smiled at him and Tracey, then turned to speak to Geraldine and Phillip.

Was she trying to set him up with Tracey? The thought spiked up his backbone, circled his skull, then needled back down, making him itch and burn. He clenched his teeth so tight he thought they'd snap.

'And the cracks are starting to show.'

'What cracks?' he demanded.

'Babies.'

He stared at her. What was she talking about?

'We don't mention babies in front of her,' Tracey said. 'Which is a bit hard, with Fran expecting her first and all.'

He fought the urge to grab her shoulders and shake some kind of rational meaning from her.

Tracey sighed. 'God, men are so thick.' She lowered her voice. 'Babies make her cry.'

Cassie never cried.

'And Cassie never cries.'

'She wants a baby? She's told you this?'

She gave him a look that told him he was

being thick again. 'And how on earth can she ever have a baby when this town has her mourning Brian for ever?'

Sol glanced at the photographs on the walls. She followed his gaze. 'Gruesome, huh?'

'She did all this after Brian died?'

'Nah, Brian did it himself, while he was still alive.' She gave a wry grin. 'My brother was a lot of things, but modest wasn't one of them.'

'You can say that again.' But there was something more—something Sol couldn't put his finger on. His eyes settled on Cassie for a moment, and for the first time he let himself wonder what her marriage had been like. Had she enjoyed being married to Brian Parker? He glanced at the walls again. Maybe it hadn't been such a bed of roses after all.

'C'mon, dinner is ready. And you're sitting next to me.'

'Is Cassie trying to set us up?' The idea set his teeth on edge again.

'I asked her to.'

He did a double-take. 'Why?'

'Because I want to find out what it is about

you, Sol Adams, that's put my father's nose out of joint big-time.'

A grim satisfaction slogged through him. It'd give him a great deal of satisfaction to make Jack Parker squirm for a bit.

Then his satisfaction fled. Cassie had agreed to set him up with Tracey? Tracey stared at him, obviously waiting for an answer. He lifted a shoulder. 'I wouldn't mind knowing that myself.'

She raised an eyebrow, but said nothing as she led him through to the dining room. He held her chair out for her, then took his own seat, and glanced up to find Brian beaming at him from the living room wall opposite.

'Will you help Cassie out with the baby thing?'

His jaw dropped. He swung to her.

She giggled. 'I didn't mean it like that.' She chuckled again, as if the idea tickled her. 'But if the town saw the two of you together—out on dates and stuff—it might get them thinking it's time for Cassie to move on.'

Cassie's face replaced Brian's as she walked

through, carrying a large bowl of salad. Anger he couldn't explain clenched through him. 'I'll see what I can do,' he managed through gritted teeth.

Tracey planted a quick kiss on his cheek and Cassie blinked, then beamed at him. It took his breath away—until he realised why. She thought her plan was working. She thought he and Tracey were a match made in heaven.

Hell.

Tracey laughed and leaned in close to Sol. It made Cassie's throat burn.

Help me through this dinner. Help me through this dinner. She repeated the words over and over in her head, praying for strength. One more course to go, that was all. Dessert. She could keep it all together for one more course, surely?

She bit back a sigh when Keith tossed a glare in Sol's direction. He and Brian had never cared for Sol. Sol hadn't played rugby. Even back then they'd sensed his indifference and resented it. Sol had been above all that. Sadness shadowed through her. He'd had bigger things to worry about.

Sol laughed his deep hot chocolate laugh at something Tracey said and Cassie leapt to her feet. 'I'll get the pie.' She managed a smile. 'If you could see to the drinks, Keith?' Then she disappeared into the kitchen before the smile slid straight off her face.

She was *jealous* of Tracey? Tracey, with her beautiful blonde hair and her beautiful blue eyes and her beautiful slim figure. Just like Jean's. Just like Fran's, if you discounted that bulge. She squished her eyes shut. She definitely had to discount that bulge.

No, no. She loved Tracey. Tracey was dearer to her than a sister. But that didn't stem the tide of dark emotion that poured through her. Sol was hers. From her old life. From before Brian, before the Parkers.

She clutched the table. *Get a grip.* Becoming a Parker had made things good.

But she remembered sitting in a tree with a boy. A perfect understanding. A perfect friendship. Ha! Or so she'd thought. Sol had upped and left without a word. Disappeared like all the other men in her life.

It'd been hard losing him like that. Harder even than—

She cut the thought off and pressed the heels of her hands to her eyes. She knew why he'd left. He'd had to. It was as simple as that. Sometimes all you got in life was one chance, and if you didn't grab it… She sighed. She and Sol, they'd taken theirs. Now all they had to do was live with them.

'Everything okay?'

She jumped and turned. Sol stood in the doorway. The faint woodsy smell of his after-shave tantalised her, made her nostrils flare as she breathed him in. 'Uh-huh, everything's fine.' She pasted on a bright smile. 'Are you enjoying yourself?'

'Yes.'

The word sounded so definite, and his eyes burned so fiercely that Cassie's chest tightened up until she thought she might never breathe properly again. 'I wasn't sure if you would.' *And she would've been wrong.* 'So, you're glad you're home for Christmas, then?'

'You bet.'

He was, huh? Did he want Tracey as a Christmas present? She gripped her hands tight in front of her. 'What do you want, Sol?'

His gaze met hers, hot and hard. Silence stretched between them. The pulse at the base of her throat fluttered to life.

'What do I want?' he finally asked in his hot chocolate voice.

She nodded. He stepped closer and her pulse didn't just flutter, it pounded.

'To see if you need a hand.'

She watched the lean, masculine line of his lips shape the words and—

Of course! She took a hasty step back. Of course. What else could he possibly want? She glanced around the kitchen. 'I…umm—' She pounced on the dessert plates and shoved them at him. 'I'd appreciate it if you'd take those through for me.'

She seized the apple pie and the bowl of whipped cream and sped back into the dining room. She glanced at Brian's picture as she passed, used it to bolster her determination, to remind herself she had everything she wanted, to draw in strength.

But it didn't help her eat apple pie.

Sol glanced at the spoonful of pie she pushed around her plate, then at her. 'It's good. You should try it.'

She managed a weak smile. 'I'm full.'

With a shrug, he turned back to Tracey.

Oh, dear Lord, would the night never end?

Phillip and Geraldine left first. Followed soon after by Sol and Tracey. It was nothing to her if Sol saw Tracey home. In fact—she gritted her teeth—it was great.

Keith stared at her morosely when she came back into the living room. It was sweet of him to play host. Real sweet. She had lots of friends. *Brian's friends,* a little voice whispered through her. She pushed it away. She wouldn't listen to it. Not tonight.

'I still don't know what you ever saw in him.'

'Sol?' She shrugged. 'He was a good friend.'

'He didn't play rugby.'

That made her grin. 'There's more to life than rugby, you know.'

Keith was silent for a few moments. 'So, he's a big-shot architect now, huh?'

She started to collect up the plates. 'Apparently.'

'Is that going to impress Tracey?'

Cassie stared at him for a moment, then set the plates down and dropped into a seat. 'You like Tracey?' How had she not seen this? She gripped the table. 'You should ask her out to dinner. Somewhere nice—not the Leagues Club.'

'Yeah, but she's Brian's little sister, and—'

'And she's twenty-six years old, between boy-friends, and she's gorgeous.'

Tracey and Keith? She should've seen it. She really should. They'd be perfect for each other.

'I'm not some big-shot architect from the city.'

'But you do run the best darn automotive shop in Schofield.'

He leaned towards her. 'You really think I should?'

'Yes!' He started at her shriek, and she forced herself to moderate her voice. Her gaze narrowed on the picture of Brian. She motioned to it. 'Brian would've given you his blessing.' He sure as heck had hers.

'Right.' Keith straightened in his chair. 'Right.' He nodded. 'Thanks, Cass.'

'Any time,' she mumbled as she led him to the door. Absolutely any time. She really didn't care that Sol had taken Tracey home. It was none of her business. Still, it wouldn't hurt him to have some competition.

And when she dropped in to see Tracey the next day she absolutely, positively didn't care that Tracey had received the biggest, reddest bunch of roses Cassie had ever seen.

She didn't care. Not one little bit.

CHAPTER FOUR

SOL drummed his fingers against his knee and watched Cassie prepare Alec's meal. He savoured the sight of her as she bustled around the kitchen. He hadn't seen her yesterday, and something told him that if she thought she could get away with it she'd slip out while he wasn't looking today too.

That wasn't going to happen. Not with a jug of Alec's homemade lemonade in the fridge. Not after Alec had told him she was particularly partial to it on these hot summer days.

Cassie placed a plate of rissoles and veggies in front of Alec. 'There.'

Man, they smelt good. Last week she'd offered to fix him a meal at the same time too, but he'd declined. Alec ate at the ridiculously early hour of five-thirty. Now he wondered if he'd been a little hasty.

Nah, he wasn't going to take advantage of her kindness. She did enough as it was.

'I'll feed the kittens and lock them up, then I'll be out of your hair.' Before she pushed out through the back door, she glanced at the kitten in Alec's lap. With a shake of her head she left it there.

Sol leapt to his feet, grabbed two glasses and the jug of lemonade and pushed out after her. 'Sit down and relax, Cassie.'

She glanced up from dishing out food for the kittens. They pushed their heads against her hands in simple adoration. Her eyes lit on the jug and he could practically see her mouth start to water. 'Oh, Sol, I have a hundred things to do today.'

He waggled a glass at her. 'You'll get through them quicker if you're not dehydrated.' She darted a quick glance at the jug again. 'And it'll only take five minutes. Besides, I want to have a word with you about Alec.'

It was a low trick, but it worked. She immediately took the seat opposite. She lifted a glass. 'Okay, fill me up, partner.'

He did, and she took a long swig. The arc of her throat formed a perfect line to her—

'What about Alec?'

He blinked, found her staring at him, and shook himself. 'Alec, uh… Can he keep that damn kitten?'

She laughed, her eyes dancing at his mixture of chagrin and exasperation.

It made him grin too. 'It's just they're inseparable.'

'Sure he can keep the kitten.' Her eyes remained on his as she raised her glass and took another sip. 'For now.'

The lemonade left a wet shine on her lips. He rubbed the back of his neck. 'Until Christmas, huh? You already have a home for it?'

'No.' She ran her finger around the rim of her glass.

'So what's the problem?' She had to see as well as he did that Alec doted on that runty bundle of mismatched fur.

'He can keep it until he goes into the nursing home. I'm sorry, Sol, I've asked but they won't allow pets.'

The nursing home. He leapt up and gripped the veranda railing. 'Why can't he stay here?'

She joined him at the railing, her violet eyes full of concern. 'He's a sick man, Sol, and we simply don't have the resources to provide him with a full-time nurse.'

He chewed over her words for a moment. 'Is it just a question of money?'

'Pretty much.'

'I can pay.'

He didn't know who was more startled by his offer—him or Cassie. But as the surprise in her eyes turned to warmth he was glad he'd made it.

'Do you mean that?'

'Sure.' Why not? He had plenty of money.

'Even though he was a terrible father?'

Her smile warmed the cold places in his heart. He stared back out over the yard, down to Cassie's tree. 'To be fair, Alec never lost it until Pearl left.' That was when the drinking had started. 'And even when he was at his worst he always gave me money to feed the kids.' Sol's brothers, Luke and Lew, were in the army now. They never came back to Schofield either.

Cassie had had to steal money from her mother's purse on benefit day to make sure there was food in the house. If she hadn't, she'd gone hungry. He remembered shoving a whole box of two-minute noodles into her arms once. It was the closest he'd ever seen her come to crying.

No wonder she'd fallen for Brian. His life must've seemed like a fairytale to her back then.

And now?

His hand clenched around the railing. Now she apparently cried at the mere mention of babies. He swung around. 'If you remarried, Cassie, you could have a baby.'

Her mouth dropped. 'I beg your pardon?' She hauled it shut again and all the lines around it went white and hard.

He rubbed a hand across his eyes. He hadn't meant to blurt it out like that. He'd meant to approach it gently, softly. He stared at her profile and his chest started to ache. She squinted, as if glaring into the sun—only the sun was behind them, not ahead.

He took her chin in his fingers and turned her to face him. 'You'd make a wonderful mother, and anyone with half a brain can see you'd love to have a baby.' Her eyes shimmered, blurred, and the ache in his chest burned harder. 'If you remarried you could have those babies.' Actually, technically she didn't have to be married, but Cassie had always been an old-fashioned kind of girl.

She unhitched her chin from his fingers. 'Drop it, Sol. I don't want to talk about this—and, frankly, it's none of your business. How did we get from kittens to babies, anyhow?'

He ignored that. '*You* don't mind your business. You see someone hurting and you jump right in. You've made things better between Alec and me. Let me help make things better for you.'

Her face closed up. 'You can't make this better.'

'You shouldn't shut yourself off from life like this,' he persisted. 'It's not healthy.'

She stilled. When she spoke her words were very deliberate. 'If you want to help me, Sol, you'll drop this.'

Not a chance. 'If I wanted to help you I wouldn't let you bottle all this up. I wouldn't let you bury yourself.' He wondered if that was true, though. He'd searched for a chink in her armour since…since her leg had dangled out of that tree five days ago. And he wasn't letting go of it now. 'A baby, Cassie,' he repeated.

Her hands shook. 'And what if I can't have a baby, Sol? Physically? What then? Do you think you can fix that?'

Her words knocked the breath clean out of his body. She pushed past him to fly down the back steps and across the backyard. Her words crashed around in his head. Accusing him. Condemning him. He dug his fingers into his scalp until it hurt. How much more proof did he need that ten years ago she'd chosen the right man?

'That wasn't well done.' He swung around to find Alec peering at him through the screen door. 'Aren't you going to go after her?'

He glared back out across the yard. 'So I can do more damage?' He was shocked by the anger in his voice. 'She won't want to see me.' Ever again.

'She's been bottling that up for a long time.'

Really? Tell me something I don't know, Einstein. He bit back the words. This wasn't Alec's fault.

'Someone needs to go after her to make sure she doesn't do something silly.'

He swung around. Silly? What did Alec mean?

'More suicides in the holiday season than the rest of the year put together,' he added cheerfully.

Sol stiffened. She wouldn't—

'And she's a nice girl. She shouldn't cry alone. You're the one who pushed, so take responsibility for it, boy.'

Alec was right. Sol vaulted the veranda railing to the yard below, then stopped. Cassie had slipped over the fence separating their yards, but her handbag and keys sat on Alec's kitchen table. If she couldn't get into her house…or her car…

He thought for a moment, and the ten years he'd been away shrank as if they'd never existed. He pressed his lips together. He knew exactly where she'd be. He set off down the driveway, turned left, and headed for the cemetery at the end of the road.

'Well done, Cassie Campbell, you idiot,' Cassie muttered, dropping to the low, sweeping branch of the weeping willow. She hid her face against its trunk and squished her eyes shut. Sheesh, talk about overreaction. Sol must think her a total fruitcake. But why, why, *why,* did he have to go and start talking about babies? It was hard enough coping with other people's babies, other people's pregnancies, but to have her own held up to her like that.

Impossible.

She dropped her head to her hands. It was nearly eighteen months. Seventeen months and eight days, to be precise. Five hundred and twenty-seven days since she'd lost her baby. Five hundred and twenty-six days since she'd screamed those accusations at Brian. Those ugly, hurtful accusations. She gulped. He'd sped away in that ridiculous Porsche and she'd never seen him again. Within the same hour he'd wrapped himself around a telegraph pole.

She hadn't told a soul about that argument.

Or about the baby.

And, God forgive her, she was glad she'd never had to clap eyes on Brian again—because he would never have been able to make that right. Ever.

But she hadn't wished him dead.

'Cassie?'

Sol! She leapt up and pushed her hair off her face.

'Don't get up.'

Warm hands on her shoulders urged her to sit again. He sat beside her. There was room for two on the branch, and its overhanging greenery provided a screen from the outside world. She'd been finding refuge here for more years than she cared to remember. The fronds moved in the breeze and she glimpsed the river in the distance.

'I'm sorry I pushed the baby issue.'

She hunched her shoulders and stared at the ground.

He was silent for a moment. 'Are you one hundred per cent certain you can't have children?'

Her lips twisted. 'You're sorry, but you're going to keep pushing, right?'

'No.'

Something about the sadness of his smile untwisted her lips, loosened the knot lodged beneath her ribcage. It wasn't idle curiosity. He was worried about her. As he'd always been.

'The doctors can't tell me for sure.' She hauled in a breath. 'Around the time Brian died I had an infection.' Her hands fluttered around her abdomen and he nodded. 'They've said I'll have…difficulty.' She glanced down at her hands. 'And to not get my hopes up.'

Sol pursed his lips. 'Difficult but not impossible?'

She shrugged. She had no intention of following that line of reasoning. That avenue was very firmly shut to her. She'd bolted the door herself.

It was for the best.

She didn't look at him. 'How'd you know where to find me?'

'A simple matter of deduction.'

She glanced up before she could stop herself, but she forgot the question on her lips and lost herself in the kindness of his eyes instead.

His woodsy scent feathered a caress across her senses. She glanced at the shadow on his jaw and her fingers curled against her palms. When she glanced back up, his eyes had darkened and her mouth went dry.

Ten years of loneliness welled up inside her.

His lips looked lean and firm, intriguing and full of promise. Her heart hammered in her ears. She swayed towards him…

Good Lord! What did she think she was doing? 'Deduction?' she squeaked, shooting back and jamming herself against the trunk. 'You knew I used to come down here?'

The pulse at the base of his jaw worked. 'Yeah.'

She gritted her teeth, tried to seize control of her heart-rate. 'How?' He'd had enough on his plate with Luke and Lew, without having kept tabs on her too.

'I used to come down here. Then you started coming.'

Understanding slammed into her. 'You left it for me?'

'I figured you needed a place just for you. A place to be alone.'

Warmth flooded her. 'I would've shared, you know.'

'It's no big thing, Cassie.'

It was to her. 'A place to be alone?' She glanced out through the leaves, then grinned.

'We couldn't have picked a better spot if we'd tried.'

Sol grinned too. 'So I can safely assume the cemetery of Schofield hasn't become a thriving metropolis over the last ten years, then?'

'Oh, no.' And for that she was grateful. 'You should cremate Alec when his time comes, so he doesn't spoil this view.'

Sol stared at her for a moment, then gave a bark of laughter.

Cassie's hand flew to her mouth. 'Not that it'll spoil my view,' she said in a rush, 'but it might spoil yours.' But only if he came down here, only if he stayed—and that was nonsense. Sol wasn't going to hang around in Schofield. He was here for a holiday. 'I cremated my mother and scattered the ashes. I didn't want her spoiling this place for me.' That was all she'd meant. She knew Sol would understand.

'So you still come here?'

'From time to time.'

'Would Alec being here spoil it for you?'

She shook her head. 'Though his death will make me sad.'

Sol was quiet for a moment. 'Is Brian buried here?'

'Over that way.' She waved her arm to the left. 'I can't see it from here, so he can't spoil it either.'

Sol leaned towards her. 'Cassie, why would Brian's grave spoil this place for you?'

She stared at him, stricken. Then turned away and closed her eyes. She could feel the warmth of his shoulder almost touching hers, and for a moment she wanted to lean into him, accept the comfort he silently offered. He made her feel safe. Safe in a way Brian never had. For a moment she was tempted to tell Sol the truth—show him all the badness inside her.

She opened her eyes and shifted away. Impossible.

'The only reason Brian's grave would spoil this place for you is if you're not over him yet. Or you are and you feel guilty about it.'

No, they weren't the only reasons.

'So, which is it?'

And she didn't want to lie to Sol about it either. She might not be able to reveal the whole truth, but she could avoid lying about it. She was tired of lying. 'Not over him or over him and guilty?' She rolled the words around in her mouth. 'If they're my only options then I guess I'd have to choose guilty.'

At least that was the truth. She met his eyes and he didn't blink. He just stared down at her with that unflinching compassion.

'I'm so over Brian,' she continued, wanting to shock him, 'you wouldn't believe it.'

'Try me.'

If possible, his eyes grew warmer. Her throat closed over for a moment, then she tossed her head. 'I'm unbelievably glad I'm no longer married to Brian, I'm ecstatic that I no longer share a house with him, and I'm over the moon that I no longer share a life with him.'

Sol's warmth, his compassion, didn't wane, and with a jolt she realised she hadn't expected it to.

'Your marriage wasn't a happy one?'

'No, it wasn't a happy marriage, Sol. It was hell.' His gentleness made her want to weep. 'The morning he died we had a fight and I told him I was leaving him.' She shrugged. 'I said a lot of seriously ugly things. Then he took off in that damn car.'

'You think he killed himself?'

'No. It was an accident caused by his recklessness. He would've been pushing that car to its limit.' She picked a piece of imaginary lint from her skirt. 'Brian's release was always physical.'

'You can't hold yourself responsible for that, Cassie. He—'

'I've gained so much through his death in every imaginable way. He had a huge life insurance policy, so I'll never have to work again. Plus the whole town loves me.' Her lips twisted. 'Some kind of grieving widow, huh?' What a fraud. 'What's even worse is his family absolutely adores me.'

'So they should.'

'They wouldn't if they knew the truth.'

'I bet they would.'

No, he was wrong there. And there was no way on God's green earth she'd risk it by putting it to the test. If they ever found out she'd meant to leave Brian they'd want to know why, and she absolutely, positively couldn't tell them that. It would hurt them too much, and they'd been through enough already.

'What went wrong with your marriage, Cassie?'

She stared at him for a moment, then uttered the words she'd never dreamed of telling another soul. 'He used to hit me.'

Sol blinked, and in that instant fury, dark and dangerous, burned in his eyes. Cassie didn't flinch. She knew it wasn't directed at her.

'It wasn't often. In over nine years of marriage he hit me six times. And only ever after he'd been drinking.' But the threat of his violence had hung over her like the sword of Damocles. She'd never known when it was going to fall.

'It was okay when he drank beer, but brandy made him mean. When he drank brandy he'd pick a fight.' And after the last time he'd hit her she'd sworn he'd never get the opportunity again.

Sol leapt to his feet, his hands clenched into fists as he paced. He swore once, loudly and succinctly.

Cassie patted the branch beside her. 'Sit down,

Sol. Brian's dead, so you can't beat him to a pulp. And even if you could I'd ask you not to. Violence doesn't solve anything. You know that. Besides…' She hauled in a breath. 'It's all over now.'

Sol crouched down in front of her. 'You deserved better than that, Cassie Campbell.' He took her face between her hands. 'Much better.'

'I'm not sure I did.' His head reared back and she could see that this time her words had seriously shocked him. 'I didn't love Brian. I thought I did when I married him, but…' She sighed as Sol sat heavily beside her again. 'I married him for his family. I mean they were the Parkers, for heaven's sake—the kind of family I'd spent my whole childhood dreaming about.'

She met Sol's gaze. 'I guess he must've worked that out. That I loved his family more than I'd ever love him.'

Sol tried to contain the anger that raged through him. He didn't want to alarm Cassie, frighten her. She'd been through enough. His hands curled into fists. She'd been through enough to last a lifetime.

'It doesn't justify him hitting you.' She had to see that. 'Nothing justifies a man hitting a woman.' Loathing, cold and hard, slid in between his ribs. He didn't care if violence solved anything or not. If Brian were alive he'd…

But not in front of Cassie. He glanced at her and his anger evaporated. He wanted to pull her into his arms and hold her safe and never let anything hurt her again.

'I didn't pick him to be the kind of man to hit a woman.' She scratched her head. 'What about you? From what you remember of Brian, would you have thought that of him?'

'No.' Not back then. He doubted the thought would've even crossed his mind. But now… He thought about her living room wall.

'So, you see why I can't get married again.'

'No!' The word broke from him, harsh and loud.

'I obviously have ridiculously poor judgement where men are concerned.' She shrugged. 'I'm not risking it again.'

'Hell, Cassie.' Despair jolted through him. 'Not all men hit women.' His lips twisted into a smile, but he knew it didn't reach his eyes. 'I'd even go so far as to say most men don't hit women.'

'And I'd believe you.'

'But?'

'But I don't trust myself to be able to pick one.'

He should've stayed and fought for her ten years ago. Fighting the living, breathing Brian would've been easier than wrestling his ghost.

She turned in her seat and met his eyes fully. 'What if there's something in me that makes men violent?'

Her words punched through him. He jumped up and sliced a hand through the air. 'You've lost the plot if that's what you think.'

A ghost of a smile flitted across her lips. 'You look as if you'd like to shake me to within an inch of my life about now.'

'Shake some sense into you,' he muttered, dropping back beside her.

'It's all academic anyhow, because it's not going to happen. I don't want a husband. I have everything I need.'

Her confidence rankled. 'Really?'

'I have the family I've always dreamed of, financial security so I never have to go hungry, and a whole town full of friends.'

Yet she thought she'd gained it all by marrying Brian, and not on her own account.

As if she could read his mind, she said, 'I don't care how I got it, Sol. I'm not letting it go.'

Didn't she see that—?

'What about you? Do you think you'll marry?'

'Yes.' The word left him before he knew it.

She leaned towards him. 'Really?'

He nodded as her fragrance curled around him.

She bit her lip then frowned. 'Do you have anyone in mind?'

'Yep.'

She leaned back. 'Tracey?'

Exhilaration sped through him when he realised she looked as nauseated as he'd felt on Saturday night.

She expelled a breath. 'I guess I'd better find a way of letting Keith down lightly, then.'

The exhilaration dissolved. 'It's not Tracey.'

She mulled that over for a moment. 'Then it has to be a girl from back home in the city.'

The city wasn't home. Schofield was.

The thought spurred him to his feet. He stalked to the edge of the space and glared out at the river. Schofield? Home? Why not? It wasn't any crazier than the other thoughts running through his head at the moment. He hauled in a breath. Goddammit, he shouldn't be thinking about marrying Cassie Campbell after all these years.

It wasn't why he'd come back.

Are you so sure? a voice taunted in his head.

No, dammit, he wasn't. But when Cassie found out what he was really doing back in Schofield he had a feeling she wouldn't give him the time of day. And that put a completely different complexion on the matter.

'I have to get going.' She leapt to her feet as if she expected him to stop her.

'Okay.'

The silence as they walked the short distance back to Alec's was tense. The Christmas lights from the tree in the living room mocked him in the early-evening light.

Christmas. Home. Cassie.

Grouped together, those words seemed cosy.

Looked at objectively—what a mess.

But it wasn't until Cassie had driven off that Sol realised how skilfully she'd directed him away from any talk about babies. What had her fight with Brian been about? Had it been about babies? He'd lay his life on a bet that it had.

And then he saw it in all its awful clarity. The punishment she'd forced on herself.

CHAPTER FIVE

CASSIE hummed as she slapped pumpkin-orange paint on the wall. Not in her wildest flights of fancy had she ever thought this place would become a haven for her. Growing up in this house hadn't been pleasant. But that had been her mother's fault.

A knock on the back door dragged her out of her reverie. Alarm spiked through her. She didn't want anyone to see what she'd done to the place. As far as anyone knew she was just slapping on a coat of paint. She bit her lip and glanced around. Somehow it had become bigger than that.

A second knock, then, 'Cassie?'

Relief surged through her. It was only Sol. 'Coming.' She dropped her paintbrush to the tray, straightened her skirt and smoothed her hair back behind her ears. 'Hi.' She peered out, hoping she didn't have paint on her face.

Sol stood there, grinning from ear to ear, a paper bag in one hand and a jug of Alec's homemade lemonade in the other. 'I brought you lunch.'

She grinned back. She could feel it reach right down inside of her. 'Still looking out for me, Sol?'

'Nah—just didn't feel like eating alone.' He hoisted the bag. 'It's only banana sandwiches.'

Cassie loved banana sandwiches. Her stomach rumbled its approval. She glanced at her watch and her eyes widened.

'Yep, two o'clock,' he confirmed. 'If you're anything like me, you lose track when you're working on a project. Gonna let me in?'

'Umm, why don't we eat out here? It's nicer, and it doesn't smell of paint.'

'But I didn't bring any glasses.' He lifted the jug.

'I'll grab some.'

'But I want to see what you've done with the place. Alec said you were redecorating.'

She snorted. 'If you call slapping on a coat of paint redecorating.'

'Are you going to let me in?'

His smile was warm and steady, and even from where she stood his scent drifted across to her, clean and cool and masculine. She stared back, then wordlessly pushed the door open.

Her knee twitched as his lean length squeezed past. He stopped halfway, at the point where his chest pressed lightly against her breasts. His eyes dropped to her lips and Cassie's heart-rate thundered in her ears.

'You look real nice, Cassie Campbell.'

She went to correct him, to tell him it was Cassie Parker, but she found she didn't have any breath in her body. Then he was past and she could breathe again.

Kind of.

He stopped and glanced around. Nerves circled her stomach like sharks. She leapt forward, took the jug and sandwiches and hitched her head in the direction of the rest of the house. 'Help yourself.' Her voice came out on a high-pitched squeak.

Sol folded his arms. Very slowly he cocked an eyebrow. 'Do I make you nervous, Cassie?'

Blood rushed to her face. 'No.' She tried to snort.

'You sound a bit…strange.'

She fanned a hand in front of her face. 'Paint fumes.'

'If you're sure…'

Indignation slugged through her. 'Of course I'm sure.'

'Good.' He rubbed his hands together. 'Because I want the grand tour from you.'

Why? The question burned her tongue. She placed the lemonade and sandwiches in the fridge and bit it back. No big deal. She wiped suddenly damp palms down her skirt. It wasn't a large house. It would take next to no time.

'As you can see, I haven't finished the kitchen yet.' She led him through to the combined dining and living room. 'This area is nearly finished. Just that wall.' She pointed to the one she'd been painting moments before. 'I'm planning on carrying the blue and orange colour scheme through to the kitchen. I'm aiming for that Italian villa kind of feel.' With a self-conscious shrug, she started down the hall. 'Down here I've—'

Sol's hand wrapped around hers, bringing her to a halt. 'What?' She wanted to shake his hand free before the temptation to lace her fingers through his became too great.

'Not so fast.' He pointed to the pictures on the walls. 'Where'd you get those?'

He didn't so much as glance at her, but his thumb rubbed back and forth across the sensitive skin of her wrist, and he stared around the room in that intense, narrow-eyed way of his, and her blood started pounding and the sharks started circling in her stomach again.

'I, uh, found the frames at a garage sale.' She tugged her hand free and folded her arms in front of her.

'The pictures were in the frames?'

'Not exactly.' She shifted from one foot to the other. He'd gone into a different mode—one she didn't recognise. Intent and assessing. She had a sudden insight into what made him so successful. She wondered if he only reserved that single-mindedness for work, or if he made love with—

Good Lord! 'I painted them,' she blurted out.

He swung to her. 'You did?'

No, no—don't look at me like that, she wanted to shout. She gulped and stared doggedly at the pictures. 'They're only *trompe l'oeil*,' she mumbled.

'And what have you done to the sofa and those chairs?'

'Restuffed and re-covered them.'

Her hands twisted together as she watched him take in the dark honey of the polished floorboards, the colourful scatter rugs. Then his eyes moved towards the hallway and heat burned high on her cheekbones. 'I'm hungry,' she suddenly declared, but Sol seized her hand as she went to move past him.

'There's only the bathroom and two bedrooms to go, right?'

Exactly!

'It won't take long, then we'll eat.'

Great. Fabulous. Wonderful. The sharks circled faster and faster. She stomped down the hall and threw open the bathroom door. Terracotta tiles.

'You tiled this yourself?'

She nodded, then spun on her heel and opened

the door opposite. Her old bedroom. It was cool and green, calm and peaceful. He shot a few questions at her. She gave cursory answers.

Her feet dragged as he pulled her towards the last door. Her heart pounded when he reached for the door handle. Her breath stopped altogether when he pushed it open.

Then time stopped.

Sol's eyes widened. He stilled on the threshold. She swallowed, then glanced around, trying to see the room as he'd see it. Oh, heavens! She pressed her hands to overheated cheeks. It was way too over the top. And way too…

Purple! Every shade from the palest lilac to midnight plum. And it all centred on one piece of furniture in the room—the king-size bed. A sheer silk canopy overhung it, highlighting the richness of the satin and velvet bedspread. Silk and satin cushions spilled across the bed, then piled up in inviting corners about the room.

Too inviting. She gulped. Too lush, too sexy. What on earth had she been thinking? What on earth would Sol think of her? She glanced up and his gaze sizzled through her.

She backed up against the doorframe, her hands behind her, gripping it for support. Slowly, oh, so slowly, he closed the gap between them. He leant his arms above her head, his forehead resting lightly against hers so she was enfolded in a space that was all Sol. Touching and yet not touching.

'I like purple,' she whispered, hoping speech would ease the tension that wrapped around them.

It didn't work.

'It's the most amazing room I've ever seen.'

His eyes held hers, and she wondered if she'd ever be able to speak again.

'I look at that room, Cassie Campbell, and I want to make love to the woman who brought it into being.'

Everything inside her clenched, electrified by his words, his scent, his chest that was only a fingertip away.

'I want to kiss you more than I've ever wanted to kiss any other woman.'

His eyes darkened and dropped to her lips. She almost moaned out loud at his intense, concentrated single-mindedness.

'I want to kiss you, then I want to flick open each of those buttons...' he eyed her blouse, then met her eyes again '...slowly.'

Heat pooled in places she hadn't known she had.

'Then I want to take your lushness...' his eyes dropped to her breasts '...in my hands.' His eyes travelled down the length of her body. 'And in my mouth and in my arms.' His eyes speared back to hers. 'And then I want to take you to places you've never been before.'

Oh, man, that sounded good. Instinct told her Sol would make an amazing lover. He'd take his time. Savour each moment. And she wanted to savour those moments with him.

But what then?

The question whispered through her. She tried to ignore it, but it stayed on the edge of her consciousness, demanding attention.

What then? Then he'd up and leave again, that was what. Leave a great, gulping hole in her life for the second time.

'You're crowding me, Sol.'

He stepped back immediately, and Cassie

turned and fled—down the hall, through the kitchen, and right out through the back door. She collapsed on the top step, gulping in great lungfuls of un-Sol-scented air.

Quiet reigned for what seemed an age, then she heard him in the kitchen behind her, bustling about. That episode obviously hadn't affected him as it had her. His legs and arms hadn't turned to jelly. He could still breathe.

So could she. She closed her eyes and concentrated. Yep, it was all coming back to her. She could do this, and—

'Cassie?'

Her eyes flew open. He stood in the doorway and she forgot how to breathe again.

'Still hungry?'

Wild thoughts gripped her, then she realised he was holding out a plate. And a glass. 'Thank you.' She took them and let her hair fall across her face.

He reappeared a moment later, carrying another plate and glass. Easing himself past her, he lowered himself to the bottom step, leaving two clear steps between them. He leaned against the railing, his profile angled towards her.

'I'm sorry for what happened in there just now.' Regret thickened his words and they pierced straight through her. 'I lost my head and—' He broke off, his face pale beneath his tan. 'That room is amazing. It blew me away.'

She couldn't answer, but she knew what he meant. Seeing him in that room…her room.

'Have you ever slept in there?'

She shook her head, not trusting herself to speak. She'd stayed overnight here several times, but she'd slept in the other bedroom—the cool green one.

They ate in silence for a while, and strangely enough it wasn't fraught or uncomfortable, but companionable. She didn't know why. After what had happened—almost happened, she corrected herself—it shouldn't have been easy being with Sol.

He drained his glass, then set it down on the step above him with a decided click. 'What you've done with the house is amazing.'

'Oh, no. I've just been pottering around.'

'I'm not giving you idle praise here, Cassie. You have a real talent.'

Her stomach performed a slow somersault. He really thought so?

'If you ever decide to relocate to the city I could get you work—' he snapped his fingers '—like that.'

She stared at him for a moment. 'You think I'm good?'

He grinned a grin big enough to encompass the whole of Schofield. 'I think you're wonderful.'

A slow burn worked its way from her neck upwards. If she gave him one sign. Just one…

Her eyes met his and Sol's gaze darkened, lowered to her lips. Cassie's eyes skittered away, but not far enough. Out of their corners she could see his hot, hungry gaze. Her stomach fluttered and flailed. When he finally swung away to stare out at the backyard the fluttering didn't stop, and Cassie had to suck in a breath because she'd run out of air.

'Building recently started on a series of boutique hotels I'm working on.'

'Uh-huh?' She bit into her sandwich and pretended nothing had happened.

'Each hotel has a honeymoon suite.'

She nodded, wondering what he was getting at.

'Would you consider decorating those rooms for me?'

Her sandwich halted halfway to her mouth. 'You can't be serious.'

'Why not?'

'But I… I mean…' Sliced banana dropped out from between her two slices of bread. She abandoned it to her plate. 'I don't have any formal qualifications or anything.'

'You don't need formal qualifications when you can do that—' he hitched his head in the direction of the house '—to a room. And I promise you'll be well paid.'

'I don't know what to say.'

He reached up and clasped her hand. 'Just promise me you'll think about it, that's all.'

'Okay.' She nodded. She'd think about it.

His smile melted her to mush. She'd think about it just as soon as she unmushed her brain.

'Christmas is just around the corner.' Cassie set her glass on the table. 'What will you and Alec do?' She stared at Sol expectantly. They'd fallen into this habit of sharing a jug of lemonade on the back veranda after she'd prepared Alec's evening meal. It was the time of day she most looked forward to.

'Do?' Sol shrugged. 'I know you're into all this Christmas stuff, Cassie, but it's just another day, you know?'

Horror shot through her. Just another day? *Not.* 'Okay, so you'll get up, have a cuppa, and then…?' He gazed back at her blankly and she sighed. 'Exchange gifts?' she offered.

'Er, yeah.'

Uh-huh—so he hadn't bought Alec a gift. 'What'll you have for lunch?'

'We'll make do with a sandwich and a beer, I guess.'

Was that what he thought? Not likely. 'Are you busy for the next couple of hours?'

'Nope. Why?'

'We're going shopping.' She stood. 'C'mon.'

'Shopping for what?'

'For some Christmas cheer, that's what.'

He eased himself to his feet, stretching, and

Cassie stared at his chest and shoulders. Her mouth watered. He grinned and she blushed. 'Guess I should go get changed, then.'

'No need. You look good to me.'

And he did too. His navy cargo shorts showed off the lean, tanned length of his legs, whilst his red polo shirt caught the chestnut highlights in his hair and set off the breadth of his shoulders. Cassie eyed the intriguing vee of hair at the base of his throat and her fingers curled. She glanced up to find him watching her.

He sent her a slow grin. 'I look good to you, huh?'

'You'll do,' she snapped, leaping up and leading the way through the house and out to her car. He made no objection when she unlocked the passenger door for him, just eased his large frame into her tiny hatchback, then reached across to unlock her door.

Brian had never let her drive. Ever. He had to be the one in control. 'You don't mind me driving?' She knew the question was revealing, but she couldn't help it.

'Nope.' He grinned at her cheerfully. 'I figure

you drive like you do everything else. Wonderfully well.'

She found herself having to blink madly. She
gulped, then tried to clear her throat.

'You can hijack me any time you like, Cassie
Campbell.'

'Parker...' She tried to correct him, but her
voice wouldn't work. Sol was eying her as if she
was a bowl of cream and he was a lean, hungry
cat. Her imagination went berserk.

His grin widened. ''Cos you look real good
to me too.'

Ten minutes later Cassie pulled into a parking
space at the shopping plaza and realised she
couldn't recall a single thing about the journey.
Nothing, that was, except the solid masculinity
of Sol beside her. She hoped she'd proved him
right. She hoped she'd driven wonderfully well.
She risked a glance at his profile. At least he
wasn't white and shaking.

No, he was bronzed and beautiful.

Oh, stop it! She pushed her door open, but
Sol's hand on her arm stayed her.

'The shops are all open.'

'Yes?' What? Did he think she'd take him shopping when they were closed?

'I thought they'd be closed this late in the evening.'

'It's the week before Christmas, Sol. Of course they're open.'

'I thought they only did that in the city.'

'I guess Schofield is catching up.'

'So we're really going shopping?'

'Yes.' Why else did he think she'd hijack him? The kiss they'd almost shared a couple of days ago swelled up around her. The world tilted to one side.

Sol eased his large frame from her car, then leaned down and stared at her. 'Coming?'

'Of course.' She practically fell out of the car, then set off in double-quick time towards the glass sliding doors of the plaza and the comfort of a crowd.

He kept easy pace beside her. 'What does buying Christmas cheer actually involve?'

He smiled down at her, his shoulders relaxed, his gait confident. He walked so differently from Brian. Brian had swaggered. That swagger had started out as a kind of joke—Hey, look at me—I'm Brian Parker, league legend. She'd laughed at the joke. Then it had become a habit. The habit had set her teeth on edge.

Sol's gait didn't draw attention, but the easy way he held his large frame, his quiet assurance, had all eyes turning to him. And to her. Unease squirmed through her when eyebrows started to rise all around her. Surely they couldn't think…?

Nonsense. Of course not. She met all raised eye-brows with one of those blithe smiles she'd become so adept at. It lowered them immediately.

'What are you doing?'

'Taking you Christmas shopping.'

His eyes narrowed. 'I… Hell, Cassie, you're not going to make me buy a Santa suit, are you?'

'Now, there's a thought.' She dismissed it a moment later. A Santa suit wouldn't hide the width of those shoulders. She doubted a hessian sack could manage that. Not that she cared whether his shoulders were hidden or not. Sol's shoulders were no concern of hers. None at all. She frowned, then remembered she was supposed to be smiling blithely at all those raised eyebrows. She smiled blithely.

'Alec would really like this.' She stopped in front of a display at the bookstore and handed Sol the latest thriller from a popular author, then continued to browse.

'You want me to buy this for him?'

That made her stop. 'It's Christmas, Sol.'

'Has he bought *me* a Christmas present?'

He wasn't asking if this was a tit-for-tat thing. She knew that. It was just the idea of Alec buying him a gift had never presented itself in Sol's mind as a possibility before. She turned back to her browsing, pretending to be occupied, but with her attention focused fully on Sol. He hesitated, then walked into the store and bought the book.

'What should I buy you for Christmas, Cassie?' he asked when he came back out.

Something slid through her stomach then cha-cha-ed up her backbone. She tried to dispel the heat that rose through her, tried to act normal. 'Oh, I wouldn't worry about that if I were you, Sol. I'm still waiting for my tree house.'

He threw his head back and laughed. Heavens. How could a girl cool down when he laughed like that?

'What's next?'

'Christmas dinner.'

He rolled his eyes and she stopped directly in front of him, forcing him to stop too unless he wanted to walk right over the top of her. 'Have you considered this may be the last Christmas you'll ever spend with your father? Maybe the last Christmas you spend in Schofield?' The words coated her tongue with the taste of bitter lemons. 'Why are you so afraid to make it good?'

'I'm not afraid.'

Her hands went to her hips. 'Then you've got into bad habits.'

One shoulder lifted. 'Maybe.'

She eyed him for a moment. 'When I was a kid I hated Christmas.' He knew why. He'd hated it too. 'But as an adult, if I don't enjoy Christmas I have no one to blame but myself.'

'Are you doing this for me, for Alec, or for yourself?'

His gaze made her want to squirm. 'Maybe for all of us.'

He stared at her for a long moment, then nodded. 'Okay.' He flung an arm around her shoulder. 'C'mon, then—lead the way.'

Pleased with such an easy victory, she did. 'Can you cook?'

'Yeah, but don't make me do a whole roast dinner from scratch.'

They compromised on a turkey roll and frozen roasted vegetables. Sol only needed to pop them in the oven, set the timer, then serve. Easy as pie. Speaking of pie… 'What would you like for dessert?'

'Dessert?' he choked, holding up all the grocery bags. 'There's only me and Alec. We're never going to get through this lot.'

Hmm, he had a point. She might have gone overboard on all the sweets and shortbread and peanuts. 'It's obligatory to stuff yourself at Christmas.'

'What are my options?' he asked on a mock sigh.

'Plum pudding.'

'Uh-huh—nice and light. Or?'

'Or I'll make you a trifle.'

'You'll make a trifle? For me and Alec?'

His smile melted her all the way to her toes. Ooh—raised eyebrow. She smiled blithely as Mrs Gardener walked by. When she'd passed she turned back to Sol. 'Sure I will.'

His eyes followed Mrs Gardener. 'Who was that?'

'One of my senior citizens' daughters-in-law.'

'Why'd you keep doing that?'

'Doing what?'

He stared at her for a moment, then his eyes gleamed. 'This is perfect for you, Cassie.' His voice carried as he towed her to a nearby dress shop window and pointed to a pastel green dress that hung there. His hand moved from her arm to the small of her back. 'You'd look gorgeous in it.'

Panic spiked through her. She glanced around and saw Mrs Gardner's eyes almost bug clean out of her head—and hers weren't the only ones.

His voice deepened. 'Let me buy it for you.'

'No!' Did he really like that dress? She looked again, then gave herself a mental slap to the back of the head.

'I'd love to buy you something pretty like that.'

Oh, no—raised eyebrows surrounded her. 'What do you think you're doing?' she whispered. He sent her a slow, crooked grin and, despite her best efforts, her heart hammered against her ribs.

'I know exactly what you're up to, Cassie Campbell.'

He whispered the words in her ear and her mouth went dry. She tried to step away, but the shopfront brought her up short. 'What are you talking about?'

'You're trying to convince everyone here that I'm one of your charity cases.'

'No, I'm—'

'And I'm not a charity case, Cassie.'

'I didn't—'

'This was your idea.'

'Yes, and—'

'So the least you can do is pretend you're enjoying my company.'

Guilt wormed through her. 'I do enjoy your company, Sol. I…'

'Yes?'

'It's just...I don't want people getting the wrong idea.'

'Which would be?'

Her mouth went dry again. 'That we're dating.'

He stared at her for a moment. 'Would that be so bad?'

A small sobbing boy wearing a Spiderman tee shirt walked straight into the back of Sol's legs, saving her from having to answer.

'Hello, there.' Sol leant down to the boy. A tear-stained face glanced up and took in first Sol and then Cassie. His face fell when he didn't recognise either one of them. 'Have you lost your mummy?' Sol asked, his voice solemn. The tear-stained face nodded.

Cassie's heart clenched. He couldn't be more than four years old. She glanced around for a frantic mother, but it was hard to see through the Christmas crowd. She knelt down beside him. She wanted to pick him up and cuddle him. She didn't. It'd probably scare the beejeebies out of the poor kid—besides she was curious to see how Sol handled the situation.

'My name is Sol, and this is Cassie.'

Sol held his hand out. The little boy hesitated for a moment, then put his own hand inside it. Sol shook it, and for the first time the little boy smiled.

'What's your name?'

'Benjamin Pickering.'

Benjamin's bottom lip started to wobble again, and Sol glanced at Cassie in panic.

'Gee, Benjamin is a very grown-up name,' she started, and the lip halted mid-wobble. 'You know what, Benjamin? I bet between us we could find your mummy?'

'You do?'

'Sure I do.' She exuded a confidence deliberately designed to put him at ease. She leaned in confidentially. 'Sol here is pretty tall, isn't he?'

Benjamin nodded.

'Now, if he were to put you on his shoulders you'd be taller than everyone else here, wouldn't you?'

Benjamin's face lit up. 'And then I could see Mummy.'

'Exactly right,' Sol agreed. 'Ready, Spiderman?'

He hoisted Benjamin up with seemingly no

effort at all. Benjamin beamed from his perch. She didn't blame him. They were fine shoulders to be perched on. She gazed at them wistfully, then shook herself. She nodded to the nearby service desk and Sol nodded back.

'What's your mummy's name?' she called up to Benjamin.

He stared back at her puzzled. 'Mummy.'

Oh, well, at least they had a surname.

'What does your daddy call her?' Sol tried.

'Angela.'

She grinned at Sol. He was brilliant.

Ten minutes later they'd reunited a very relieved mother with a far from concerned son. He'd been having way too much fun on Sol's shoulders to start fretting again. It hadn't occurred to Cassie before, but Sol would make a great father.

A shaft of pain scored right across her heart, taking her completely off-guard. It was a new pain, entirely alien, and for once it had nothing to do with the fact she'd never have a child of her own but everything to do with the fact that she'd never see Sol's children. When he left, she might never see Sol again.

CHAPTER SIX

SOL glanced down at Cassie and rubbed the back of his neck. She'd been quiet since Mrs Pickering had claimed Benjamin, but at least she'd stopped all that inane smiling. 'Have we finished shopping?'

'We have.'

'Then the least you can do is let me buy you dinner.'

'Oh, Sol, that's not necessary. I—'

'Besides, I'm famished.' He took her arm and led her out through the front entrance then straight across the road and into the Leagues Club.

Cassie froze against him, then tugged her arm free. He realised his mistake too late. He shouldn't have done this. Not the Leagues Club. Not Brian's territory. He should have led her to one of the little cafés in the shopping centre, or the Chinese restaurant down the road. Not the Leagues Club.

Idiot!

He wanted to take her hand in his and soothe her. A picture of Brian smirked down from the wall. He took in Cassie's unease, glanced at the picture again, and wondered if he was really all that different from Brian after all. Everything inside him rebelled at the thought.

No, no. All he'd done was drag her off for dinner.

But he hadn't given her a chance to refuse. And she didn't want to be here. Bile rose in his throat.

'Hi, Cassie.' The girl at the reception desk waved to them. 'We haven't seen you for a while.'

Violet eyes glanced into his, and ˙anger simmered behind the rabbit-caught-in-head-lights glare. Then it was all gone, hidden. Replaced with a smile. One of those inane, set-your-teeth-on-edge smiles. His heart kicked against the walls of his chest in protest.

'Hi, Nessa. Do you remember Sol Adams?'

'Sure I do.' The perky blonde eyed him up and down, then raised a flirtatious eyebrow. 'My, my, you've certainly changed. I always wondered what happened to you.'

Garbage. Girls like Nessa here wouldn't have given him the time of day ten years ago. But he knew how the rumour mill worked in a place like Schofield. They'd all ooh and aah over his success, speculate how much he was worth.

'You remember Nessa Williams?'

He forced a smile. 'Sure—nice to see you again, Nessa.'

Nessa raised an eyebrow, and that smile flitted across Cassie's face again. It irked him as nothing else had done since he'd returned to Schofield. It told the person who received it that the bearer had nothing to hide. Yeah, sure, there might be a man by her side, but it didn't mean anything, there was a perfectly innocent explanation.

He didn't know how a smile could say so much, but it did. And it had lowered all those raised eyebrows in two seconds flat. Maybe that was what really irked him.

Just in case Nessa hadn't got the message, though, Cassie leaned in closer. 'I've been helping Sol with his and Alec's Christmas shopping.'

Light dawned in Nessa's eyes. 'Alec is one of your senior citizens, isn't he?'

Cassie nodded. 'Sol is buying me dinner as a thank-you.'

Nessa smiled as if it all made sense. Sol wished it made sense to him.

'What he doesn't know yet is that I have a secret agenda.'

Nessa's eyes widened. Sol's stomach clenched.

'I want to talk him into helping out at the nursing home do on Christmas night.'

Nessa's smile widened.

'What are you up to then, Nessa? It should be fun, and we need all the volunteers we can get.'

Nessa leaned back so quickly Sol thought she might fall off her stool. In other circumstances he'd have laughed. He didn't now, though. It was all he could do to keep the scowl off his face.

'I have family commitments,' Nessa mumbled,

then pasted on a big fake smile. 'Enjoy your meal. I hear the fish is really good tonight.'

'Great—thanks.' Cassie turned towards the bistro.

'Cassie!' A well-built man in a suit bore down on them and Sol's teeth clenched. Hell, couldn't you go anywhere in this town without Cassie being stopped, observed, hailed, watched? How could she stand it? Something darker kicked through his gut when the man leant down and kissed Cassie's cheek. Sol moved in closer, just so the other man knew he and Cassie were together. She shot him another glare, but he didn't back off.

'Garry, this is Sol Adams. We went to school together.'

The other man held out his hand, interest alive in his face. 'Nice to meet you.' Sol shook it.

'This is Garry Fraser. He came to Schofield six years ago to run the Leagues Club.'

'I'm glad you dropped by, Cassie. There's something I want to speak to you about.' He darted a quick glance at Sol. 'But I wouldn't want to interrupt, so maybe you could come by one day next week?'

Sol checked a snort. *Wouldn't want to interrupt,* my foot.

'You're not interrupting, Garry.' She launched a smile at the other man that had Sol's hands clenching.

Garry hesitated, then shot a glance at Sol as if hoping for an ally. He cleared his throat. 'As you know, Brian was the biggest rugby star to ever come out of this district.'

Sol wanted to walk away.

'We'd really like to set up a display in the club honouring his achievements. Something everyone can share.' He cleared his throat again. 'I know you have a lot of memorabilia, and I wondered if you'd consider donating it to the club? Or just lending it to us?'

Sol glanced at Garry. He'd misjudged him. He was a great guy. 'That's a brilliant idea.'

Cassie's glare told him to keep his nose out. Then she bit her lip. 'I'd have to talk to Brian's family.'

Garry raised his hands. 'Just think about it, okay?'

'Okay.'

You bet she would. Sol wouldn't let her forget.

The bistro was crowded, and as Cassie wove her way through the throng she waved and smiled at various patrons before dropping into a seat at a table on the far wall. Sol had a feeling that if one of the occupied tables had had two spare seats Cassie would have claimed them, forcing him to eat his dinner with a bunch of Brian fanatics. It would've served him right too. One look at her face told him not to dive in and tell her to hand over every last piece of Brian's football memorabilia to the club either.

Softly, softly, Adams, he told himself.

'What was all that about with Nessa?' he demanded. 'Why'd you feel the need to justify having dinner with me?'

Damn. What had happened to softly, softly? He'd meant to apologise, not—

'You already know I don't want anyone to think we're dating,' she shot back. 'This is my town, Sol. You'll be gone in another week or two. You—' she leaned across the table '—are not going to ruin what I've built up here with these people. Got it?'

He held up his hands. 'I—'

'I don't want to be here. I didn't agree to dinner.'

'We can leave.'

'Yeah, right.' She leant back arms folded. 'If I leave now everyone will think it's because you're hassling me, and with my luck you'll end up with a lynch mob on your doorstep at midnight.'

The cold places inside him started to warm up. 'And you don't want the town beating up on me, huh?'

Her face hardened. 'I've had enough of men pushing me around, Sol.'

The warm places froze over. 'I'm sorry.' Her face didn't soften. He wanted to reach across the table and take her hand. A quick glance around told him he couldn't. Too many eyes watching. 'The moment I dragged you in here I knew it was a mistake.' She lifted her chin, watching, waiting. 'I just didn't know if dragging you back out would've made it better or worse.'

'Why drag me anywhere?' she demanded. 'Why not ask, like any normal, civilised person?'

He fiddled with a tiny packet of salt. 'I've had a fun evening. I didn't want it to end. I thought if I gave you time to think about it you'd find an excuse to cry off.'

She raised an eyebrow and he nodded.

'It wasn't fair.' He stared down at the packet of salt, turning it over and over. 'When we first walked in and I saw that picture of Brian on the wall, all I could think was, I'm as bad as him.'

'No!' The word sounded her shock. She touched his hand 'You're nothing like him.'

But he'd forced her into this place and—

He met her gaze and relief pounded through him. In her eyes, at least, he wasn't another Brian. He turned his hand over and laced his fingers through hers. Her fingers were long and tapered, the fingernails painted a pale pink, her skin smooth where his thumb ran back and forth across it. Her hand trembled in his and he tightened his grip momentarily. 'You said you weren't going to let me ruin what you've built up here.'

She lifted her chin. 'I won't.'

Admiration rocked through him. She wouldn't

let herself be pushed around any more. He respected that, but… 'What you've built up here, Cassie, is a lie. You're letting these people think what you and Brian had was wonderful.'

She tugged her hand free. 'It's a good lie,' she hissed.

'It's a big lie.'

'It's made a lot of people feel good.'

'And it's put you on a pedestal.'

'So?'

He shrugged. 'So, it gets lonely up there.'

Her jaw dropped. 'You don't know what you're talking about. I'm surrounded by people who care for me.'

'Do you really believe that? Or do you think it's Brian they care about?' Her eyes skittered away but he pushed on. 'And have you stopped to wonder if you're making it harder for his family? If keeping Brian so alive and fresh in everyone's mind mightn't let them move on as they should?'

Pain tightened her face. Not for the first time, Sol wondered if he should leave her be. He glanced around and his jaw clenched. No! What would she have if all this came crashing down?

Couldn't she see it was time to stop punishing herself? 'Do you really want to live in Brian's shadow for the rest of your life?'

'You promised me dinner.' Her anger simmered again. 'Not a lecture.'

'If all these people here thought we were dating it'd take you out from under that shadow.'

'We're not dating,' she snapped. 'I'll have the fish and a Coke, thank you.'

'If I kissed you right now they'd think we were dating.'

Her mouth dropped and her bottom lip swelled, and for a moment all Sol could do was stare as desire clenched its need around him. He was transported back to the afternoon they'd shared at her house, to her beautiful erotic bedroom. All the images he'd done his best to stamp out then clamoured through him now.

'It's real lonely up there on that pedestal, Cassie. It doesn't have to be.'

She snapped back as if his words had slapped her. 'If you kiss me, Sol Adams, I'll never forgive you—and you'll have that lynch mob on your doorstep before you can count to ten.'

A slow smile spread through him. 'You wouldn't call the lynch mob on me, Cassie.' He picked up her fist, which lay on the table, and uncurled her fingers, smoothing them out between both his hands. 'I think you'd like me to kiss you.' He lifted it, unresisting, to his lips and placed a slow, lingering kiss into its palm, curling her fingers back over it before he released it. 'But don't worry. I promise not to kiss you until you kiss me first.'

'Don't hold your breath.'

He chuckled. Her eyes were so wide a man could fall into them. 'I never got you out of my head, Cassie Campbell. Not in ten years. You were the best friend I ever had.'

'Then why'd you leave like that? Without a word to me?'

Her eyes shimmered, and he wished he'd done things differently, wished he'd stayed and fought for her. He stared down at his hands and salt spilled all over his fingers from the mangled packet. 'Because you were going to marry Brian and I couldn't stand the thought of you with him.'

Her jaw dropped, her eyes darkened, then her mobile phone started to ring.

Sol silently cursed it.

'Hello?' Cassie held the mobile to her ear.

'Cassie, it's Jean. Is everything okay, dear?'

No, it's not. 'Yes, of course it is. Why shouldn't—?'

Guilt hit her right between he eyes. 'Omigod— it's Thursday night.' *Family night at the Parkers.*

'Yes, dear.'

'Oh, Jean, I'm so sorry. I've got all caught up in the Christmas thing and…' She closed her eyes. She loved Jean. Maybe more than she'd loved her own mother. Shame slugged through her. She shouldn't have neglected her like—

'It's not easy for you, is it, Cassie? This time of year?'

More guilt pounded through her. 'No.' It wasn't easy. Especially this Christmas. 'Nor for you,' she murmured. Was Sol right? Was she making it harder for Jean and Jack to move on? 'I need to talk to you and Jack about something,' she said with sudden decision.

'We're here whenever you need us. You know that.'

Yes, she did. 'I'm at the Leagues Club with Sol.' She held her breath, wondering how Jean would take that. She tried to ignore Sol, aware of how closely he followed the conversation.

Jean didn't pause. 'Why don't you come round after your meal? We've Jack's angling club and Tracey's photography club both coming for Christmas drinks.'

Cassie glanced at her watch. 'Sure, that'd be great.'

Sol gripped her hand. 'Invite me,' he mouthed.

She rolled her eyes and went to shake her head, then paused. She didn't know if she was still cross with him or not, but he had admitted he didn't want the evening to end. Strangely enough, neither did she. She pulled in a breath. 'Is it okay if I bring Sol along?'

There was an infinitesimal pause on the other end of the phone, then Jean said, 'Of course. That would be lovely.'

Jean met them at the front door. 'Cassie, dear.' She enfolded her in a hug, then held her at arm's length and gazed at her. 'My, you're looking well.'

Cassie fidgeted under the maternal gaze. She motioned to Sol.

'Sol Adams.' Jean moved forward to clasp Sol's hand in both her own. She stared up at him for a moment, sighed, then shook her head. 'My, you're a fine-looking man.'

There was a light in Jean's eye that Cassie had never seen before. Oh, Lord, she hoped Jean didn't think Sol was the reason she looked so well. Sol grinned back, not the least perturbed by Jean's scrutiny.

'I remember you, you know? You were a nice boy—quiet, but kind. I always hoped a little of what you had would rub off on Brian.'

Cassie's jaw dropped. Sol shifted beside her. 'Brian and I were very different,' he finally said.

'Oh, I think you'll find you had a lot more in common than either one of you ever thought.' Her glance shifted to Cassie. 'But what am I doing, keeping you out here like this? Come in.'

Two things struck Cassie immediately when she entered. The first, the bulge that was Fran's belly had grown alarmingly in the last week. The second, the way Tracey's face lit up when she spied Sol. She raced over, eyes sparkling, and something shifted inside Cassie.

'C'mon—I'll get you a drink.' Tracey took Sol's arm. 'Don't worry,' she added, when he glanced at Cassie. 'Cassie won't mind if I steal you—will you, Cassie?'

'Of course not.' She snorted, as if it were the craziest question she'd ever heard.

'Good—come and meet Dad.'

Cassie's snort turned into a cough. What? Tracey knew how Jack felt about Sol, so why would she…? To annoy him, that was why. A more difficult question to answer, though, was why the space Sol had taken up by her side had suddenly become a great gaping hole.

Keith sidled up and nudged her. 'What's Tracey up to, Cass?'

His words were low, and her chest clenched in sympathy. She followed his eyes to where Sol and Tracey stood, their heads cocked at the same angle, their shoulders slightly hunched.

'I did what you said. I asked Trace out and we had a great time.'

'That's fabulous.' Her eyes drifted back to Sol.

'And now she's all over this Adams guy.'

Cassie watched for a moment, then frowned. 'She's not, you know.' She had no idea what Tracey was up to, but it wasn't that. She let out the breath she'd unconsciously held.

Keith shifted beside her. 'Well, then, he's all over her and she doesn't mind—which is the same thing.'

'No, he's not.' She leaned in closer to Keith. 'They're not the least bit interested in each other. Not romantically, at least,' she qualified. A weight lifted from her. Keith opened his mouth but she cut him off. 'You trust me, don't you?'

'Sure I do.'

'Then trust me on this. They're up to something, but it's not that.'

He stared at her for a moment, then nodded. 'Okay.'

On impulse she reached up and kissed his cheek. Keith acted like a big macho bulldog most of the time, but he had a heart of gold. He deserved to be happy. 'Who knows?' She glanced back at Sol and Tracey and something tugged at her consciousness, then slipped out of reach. 'Maybe they're planning some Christmas surprise?'

She should've believed Sol when he'd said he wasn't interested in Tracey. Heaviness settled back over her when she remembered why—his girl in the city. Indignation shot through her. How come he had flirted with her tonight, then?

Her heart burned. He hadn't really flirted with her, though, had he? He'd been trying to make a point. She turned and almost bumped into Jack, a newly opened bottle of champagne in his hand. Pleasure lit his face when he saw her. It froze in the next instant when he glanced past her.

Cassie swung around to find Tracey practically glued to Sol's arm, a grin as wide as the Cheshire cat's stretched across her mouth. She waved her empty champagne flute at her father. 'Come and see who's dropped in.'

Jack stared at Sol as if he'd seen a ghost. Sol drew himself up, a challenge in his eye. The whole episode lasted all of five seconds, but it left Cassie reeling. Jack shoved the bottle of champagne into Keith's hands with a curt, 'Top everyone up for me, will you, Keith?' Then he spun on his heel and stalked from the room.

'Drink, Cassie?'

'Uh—no thanks. I want to check if Jean needs a hand with anything. Tracey's glass needs topping up, though.' She pushed him in Tracey's direction, then followed Jack.

When Cassie walked into the kitchen, Jean broke off whatever it was she was saying. Jack leaned his hands against the far countertop, his shoulders hunched, his back to Cassie. He didn't turn around and Cassie's hands twisted together. 'I shouldn't have brought Sol, should I?'

'Of course you should've,' Jean said. Her smile, though, was strained. 'It's this time of year, dear. It's…'

'I know.' Acid rose in her throat when she remembered Sol's accusation at the Leagues Club.

'Sol isn't the problem,' Jean sighed.

'Not a problem?' Jack swung around. 'He's out there making eyes at my daughter.'

Relief sped through Cassie. Since Brian had

died Jack had become increasingly over-protective of all his children, especially of his youngest. At least Cassie could set his mind at rest over that one. Tracey and Sol weren't—

'Nonsense,' Jean said crisply. 'I think you'll find he's making eyes at your daughter-in-law.'

Cassie blinked. 'Oh, no,' she denied quickly. 'There's nothing going on between me and Sol.'

'That's a shame, dear.'

Cassie wasn't sure whose jaw hit the ground first, hers or Jack's.

'Now, I believe you had something you wanted to speak to us about, dear?'

Cassie roused herself. 'Maybe now isn't the best time—'

'No, it's fine.'

Jean sat, then pulled Jack down to the chair beside her. Cassie dropped into the one opposite. She forced herself to remember Sol's accusation. It gave her the strength to continue. 'Garry Fraser made a request to me this evening on behalf of the Leagues Club.' She almost smiled when Jack straightened. After his family, rugby league was his passion.

'Yes, dear?'

'They want to set up a special display in Brian's honour.'

Jack's chin lifted, pride burning deep in his eyes. Jean's smile turned wistful. She reached out and clasped Cassie's hand. Cassie took a deep breath. 'He asked if I'd consider donating Brian's rugby memorabilia to the club.'

Jean's hand tightened. 'Do you have a problem with that?'

'No, not at all.' Then she suddenly realised how that must sound. 'I mean, I don't need all of his things around me to remember him,' she amended hastily.

Jean patted her hand. 'I know what you mean.'

'But before I do anything I wanted to find out how the two of you feel about it. Maybe there are things you'd like to keep for yourselves, or have kept in the family, or…'

She gulped. All this time she'd thought she'd been making things easier for Jean and Jack by keeping Brian's memory alive, but maybe Sol was right—maybe she'd only made it harder. Maybe she'd made it impossible for them to move on. It had made things easier for her, though. It had kept her anger at Brian alive, had strengthened her resolve never to marry again. The thought shook her.

'I know this is hard on you, Cassandra.'

'It's been hard on you and Jean too. I don't know if it's fair of me to ask this of you, Jack, but would you take care of it? You'd know exactly what the club is after. I mean, if you don't want to—'

'I'd be honoured, Cassie.'

He reached out and clasped her hand, and she knew by the way he'd used the shortened version of her name how moved he was. A weight lifted from her. 'Thank you.'

He squeezed her hand, then pushed back his chair. 'I'd better be getting back to my guests.'

Jean hugged her. 'Thank you, Cassie, dear.' Then she followed him out of the room.

'Oh, good. I've found you.' Fran collapsed in the seat beside her.

Cassie tried to smile, tried to avoid focussing on Fran's bump.

Fran turned to face her fully. She seized both

of Cassie's hands in her own. 'Cassie, you know I love you like a sister, don't you?'

'Of course I do.'

Fran's hands became urgent. 'I know my pregnancy is hard on you, but please promise me you'll love my baby.'

Cassie's jaw dropped. Then horror shot through her. 'Of course I'll love your baby, Fran. How could I not? And—'

'You can hardly stand to look at me, and in another two weeks I'll have a baby.'

Oh, God. Cassie's eyes filled. She forced the tears back. She couldn't cry. She wouldn't.

'And maybe you won't be able to stand to look at me or my baby then either.'

'No.' She hugged Fran tightly. She had to make this right. Fran didn't deserve this. 'I can't lie to you, Fran. I so wish it were me having a baby. And it's hard seeing this—' she motioned to Fran's bump '—and knowing—'

She broke off, then gave a tremulous smile. 'Oh, Fran, I swear I'll love your baby. I'm sorry you thought otherwise.'

Whatever Fran saw in Cassie's eyes made her

smile back. 'Then promise me you'll be my baby's godmother.'

Tears welled again. 'I'd be honoured.'

Fran hugged her close for a moment, then drew back, her smile brilliant. 'You don't know what this means to Claude and me.' She got to her feet as quickly as her condition allowed. 'I can't wait to tell him.'

Cassie turned to watch Fran leave and found Sol standing in the doorway. He leaned casually against the doorframe, but there was nothing casual about the way he watched her.

She swallowed. 'You heard all that?'

He nodded.

She stood, then didn't know what to do. Sol held his arms out and she didn't hesitate—she walked straight into them.

CHAPTER SEVEN

CASSIE brushed a hand down her skirt, took a deep breath, then rang the doorbell. Her stomach clenched as footsteps approached. The door opened.

'Merry Christmas, Sol.' She'd meant it to be a cheerful Santa-style greeting, but when she saw him framed in the doorway her chest tightened, her throat contracted and it came out a breathy whisper.

'Merry Christmas, Cassie.' He pushed the door open for her. 'That Santa hat is starting to grow on me.'

That's right. Santa hat. Christmas, remember? Ho, ho, ho!

Grin, she ordered herself. She hesitated in the doorway, wondering if she should kiss Sol. Just a friendly peck on the cheek in honour of the day.

But she hesitated too long and the moment passed. She clutched the trifle to her chest as she edged past him. 'Where's Alec?'

'In the kitchen.'

She started towards it, but his hand on her arm stayed her. Her stomach flip-flopped.

'I spoke to Alec's doctor and we've organised for Alec to stay at home for the time being. A nurse will start in the New Year.'

'You've arranged that already?'

'I wanted to get it sorted.'

Man, when he smiled like that he could give a girl a heart attack or—

Why had he wanted to sort it so quickly?

The warmth that had flooded her turned to ice. Because he'd be leaving soon, that was why. Schofield wasn't his home any more. And he had his girl back in the city, remember? He was probably itching to get back to her.

'So about that kitten, Cassie? Can he keep it?'

She forced the edges of her mouth upwards in one of those blithe smiles. 'Sure he can.' Then she spun on her heel and headed once more towards the kitchen. She had to get over this somehow. In another day or so Sol would be gone, and maybe she wouldn't see him for another ten years.

Unless Alec died in the interim and Sol came back for the funeral. But then, Sol didn't do funerals, did he?

'Are you okay, girlie?'

Cassie blinked to find Alec staring at her in concern. She shook herself. 'Of course I'm okay.' She smiled her Santa smile. 'I've been going a hundred miles an hour all morning, and if I don't stop soon I'm going to crash.'

'Then you better get some of this into you.' He held up a jug of eggnog.

'Ooh, yes, please—but let me feed the kittens first. I want them settled before I leave.' A shadow passed across Alec's face. 'Here's your trifle, and here's some fruitcake.'

'Lord, Cassie.' Sol stared at the dish of trifle. 'That'll keep us going for a week.'

Did that mean he'd be staying for at least another week? Her Christmas spirit magically returned. She lifted a lofty nose. 'I make one mean trifle, Sol Adams. I bet there'll be none of this left in two days.'

'You're on.'

'You find a spot in the fridge for the trifle,' she ordered Alec, 'and Sol can help me with the kittens.' She led Sol out to the back. 'Where's Rudolph?' she whispered. He hadn't been in his usual spot on Alec's lap.

'Alec put him out here first thing this morning.'

Cassie understood. It would've been too hard for Alec to actually hand the kitten over. Funny how such a little bundle of fur could burrow its way into your heart like that. 'Then the sooner we put him out of his misery the better. Here.' She handed the kitten to Sol and whipped out a length of red satin ribbon from her pocket. She quickly tied a large bow around the kitten's neck.

Sol surveyed her warmly.

'What?' She touched a hand self-consciously to her face.

'Thank you.' He took her hand and squeezed it. 'This will mean a lot to Alec.'

She swallowed. Crouched over the kitten like

this, she could see Sol's lips, tantalisingly near. She'd scoffed when he'd told her he wouldn't kiss her until she kissed him first. She wasn't scoffing now. Drought-breaking lips, that was what they were. She could break her drought on those lips and—

She stood abruptly, fighting for air. She wasn't breaking her drought. She wasn't breaking anything.

He knew. She could see it in his eyes as he slowly straightened too. He knew she'd wanted to kiss him. Heck, it wouldn't take a rocket scientist to figure that one out. His bulk stood between her and the door. He handed her the kitten and automatically she took it, but its small weight offered her little protection from the man in front of her.

He reached out a finger and traced it along her jaw and down her throat to where her pulse beat furiously. 'What you're doing isn't healthy, Cassie.'

She fought the urge to arch against that finger—fought the urge to lean into Sol as she had the other night at the Parkers. Then he'd offered her comfort; today he offered her something far more exciting.

And far more dangerous.

She gathered the kitten close, snuggling it under her chin. 'It's Christmas, Sol.'

He stared down at her for a moment, then let his hand drop. She read the message in his eyes. For now. He'd let the subject drop for now. Because it was Christmas.

He stood aside and she practically sprinted past him and back into the kitchen. Alec glanced up. 'Merry Christmas, Alec.' She kissed his cheek and placed the kitten in his hands.

'For me?'

He blinked, and Cassie's eyes misted over. She swallowed, knowing Alec disliked overt displays of emotion. 'Uh-huh.'

He seized her hand. 'Thank you.' Emotion thickened his voice. 'This is the best Christmas I can remember.' He dropped her hand to lift up the book that lay across his lap. 'See what the lad gave me?'

'That's great.' Good Lord, was Alec actually smiling? Sol entered the room. 'And what did you get Sol?'

'Oh, no, no.' His smile widened into a grin. 'You youngun's are like bulls in china shops at Christmas, wanting everything at once. It can wait till later.'

She glanced at Sol, intrigued. He shrugged back.

'Time for breakfast,' Alec ordered. 'Eggnog and fruitcake. After all, it is Christmas.'

'It is at that,' she agreed. Far be it from her to crush Alec's Christmas spirit. She raised her glass, 'Merry Christmas.' Sol and Alec clinked glasses with her, but it was the heat in Sol's eyes that stayed with her.

'Has the lad shown you your Christmas present yet?'

Cassie choked on her eggnog. Sol had a present for her? She tried to stamp out the crazy swirl of excitement that fizzed through her. 'You got me a present?'

He ginned that lop-sided grin that did strange things to her insides. He reached across, plucked the glass out of her hand, then wrapped his fingers around her wrist and pulled her to her feet.

'Close your eyes,' he ordered.

She obeyed instantly, then kinked one open again as he led her out through the back door. 'Where are you taking me?'

'No cheating. You're supposed to keep your eyes closed.'

'But—'

Laughter gurgled out of her as he tugged her Santa hat down over her eyes. It petered out as both his hands trailed down her face, cupping it and lifting it towards him.

'What are you doing?' The words were nothing more than a breath of air as the strangest fancies played through her mind. Fantasies of Sol kissing her, of being naked and blindfolded with Sol.

Oh, dear Lord, help her. She reached up to tug off the Santa hat, but Sol grabbed her hands. 'Just making sure you can't see. Now, behave.'

Behave!

'And humour me.'

She wondered how humoured he'd be if she told him what was flashing through her mind. He led her down the steps. Would he be shocked? She followed him across the yard, too caught up in her thoughts to heed where they were going.

No, Sol wouldn't be shocked by the explicitness of her fantasies. He'd grin that grin and set about bringing those fantasies to heat-searing life. Everything inside her clenched to a stop. Then she realised Sol had stopped too.

'Ready?'

No. Yes. She didn't know.

He tilted her head upwards again. Her heart started to pound in excitement, in anticipation…

'*Voilà!*'

He whisked off the Santa hat with a flourish and Cassie found herself staring up into her tree…at a tree house. She blinked. Then blinked again. Sol had built her a tree house? Her chest tightened; her throat thickened.

'What do you think?'

She heard the uncertainty in his voice but she couldn't speak. She turned, letting her eyes speak for her.

He grinned and motioned to the ladder. 'After you.'

She needed no second bidding. Her heart

expanded when she reached the top. Sol had built a simple platform with benches that ran around two of its sides. Another ladder stretched down into her yard on the other side of the fence.

She sat on one of the benches, her eyes shining as she took in the view. Smiling, she finally turned to Sol, sitting quietly on the other bench watching, his knee nearly touching hers. 'It's fabulous,' she whispered.

'It's not nearly as fancy as my original plans of ten years ago.'

'I think it's perfect.'

Regret pierced her in the next moment. 'I didn't get you anything, Sol.' She should've got him something. She stared at him stricken. 'I'm sorry—'

He reached across and laid a finger against her lips. 'You've already given me more than enough, Cassie. You've helped ease the way between Alec and I. You've brought us more than trifle and fruitcake today. You've brought us Christmas.'

'That's nothing more than being a friend.'

He eyed her for a moment then grinned that

crooked half-grin. 'Then I guess you could give me a Christmas kiss, as one friend to another, and we'll call it even.'

As one friend to another? His eyes held hers and she knew she couldn't refuse. Bracing her hands on his knees, she leant across and pressed her lips to his. A sigh breathed out of her as his scent engulfed her. Her lips clung to his for a fraction longer than they should have, then she pulled back and sat, hands demurely folded in her lap. 'Merry Christmas, Sol.'

'You just kissed me, Cassie.'

The obviousness of that made her grin. 'Yes, I did.'

She gasped when he picked her up and set her in his lap. One of his arms went around her shoulders; his other hand gripped her chin. 'I can kiss *you* now.'

'Wha—?'

Her throat closed over at the look in his eyes.

'I told you I wouldn't kiss you until you kissed me first.'

But she hadn't kissed him like that! Not romantically. Not—

'And I'm going to kiss you, Cassie. Like I should've kissed you ten years ago.'

His lips descended to hers—not quickly, not slowly, but with determination. She watched, frozen, seconds stretching into something beyond time. Struggling didn't enter her head. All her limbs turned to liquid in that half-second before contact, then his lips claimed hers.

They weren't tentative and they weren't tender. They were forceful and demanding. They didn't hurt her, but they drank from her deeply, as if they needed whatever she could give. And as if they had no intention of ever stopping.

Cassie didn't have the strength to pull back. She didn't even have the thought as sensation pounded through her. He demanded and she gave. She could only do as his lips, his hands, his tongue bade her.

She was putty, she was helpless, and she gave and gave. Opening her lips as his tongue demanded, opening herself as he demanded, and he drank and drank until he reached her very soul, and there was nothing but her and her soul to give, and he kept drinking until a moan wrenched out of her, dredged up from some place so deep she thought she'd drown.

Only then did he lift his lips, and she dragged in great gulps of air. The darkness, the fierceness of his eyes held her still.

'I'm not going to apologise for that,' he growled, hoisting her in his arms so she sat rather than lay in his lap. 'And I'm going to kiss you again, Cassie Campbell.'

He didn't give her time to respond. Clasping her face in both his hands he pulled her lips against his in a hard kiss that had the blood stampeding through her veins. It spoke of the frustration of a long wait and of the exhilaration now. Again Cassie felt powerless against it, swept along by his hunger.

Then in the blink of an eye it changed. Lips and hands gentled and teased as kisses were pressed to the corners of her mouth, to her eyelids. Fingers raised gooseflesh on her arms as they trailed a path down her throat and along her collarbone. Kisses that played and asked her to play, kisses that slowly created a heat and need deep inside her until she'd thought she'd die if they didn't deepen and give her what she needed.

But they evaded all her attempts until, with a groan, she straddled Sol's lap and with both hands held his head still and met his lips fully with her hunger. For one electrified minute he stilled beneath her, then his arms crushed her to him as he matched her hunger. Her last rational thought before her mind fogged over was—*I am home.*

Sol breathed her name over and over between kisses, breaking off to press scorching lips to her neck. His fingers slipped under her blouse, fanned over her ribs, tantalised the underside of her breasts. She moaned as his thumbs found her nipples and urged them to stark desire. Then her breasts spilled free.

'Oh, God, I've died,' she almost sobbed.

'Not died,' he whispered, pushing her blouse up. His tongue flicked across a nipple. 'You're coming back to life.'

She shuddered as his breath whispered across the wetness of her skin, then cried out and arched against him as he took the engorged bud in his mouth and circled it with his tongue. Her fingers dug into his shoulders and she pushed herself against the bulge in his lap. She couldn't help it. Some power greater than herself had hold of her.

'Cassie, in another moment I'm not going to be able to stop.'

Stop? Who said anything about stopping? She moved against him again and a shudder racked through him. She wanted to make him shake and tremble. She wanted to make his knees as weak as hers. She wanted him to want her so much it hurt.

Pulling back, she gazed into his eyes and raked her fingers down his chest to the waistband of his shorts. Her lips descended towards his. Sol twisted her hair around his hand and held her back. Her eyes dropped to his lips; her own lips parted. 'Kiss me, Sol.'

With a muffled oath he drew her down to kiss her. When he drew back Cassie had to blink to clear her vision.

'I meant what I said, Cassie. In another moment I'm going to lose all control.'

She gazed at his mouth and her lips parted in anticipation. He tugged on her hair, forcing her to meet his eyes. 'I don't have any protection with me, Cassie. Do you understand?' He gave her a little shake. 'Because in another moment I'm not going to care.'

Slowly his words reached through the fog clouding her brain. *Omigod!* She pushed him and the hand on her hair fell away, but the one at her waist held her fast.

'Let me go,' she breathed in a furious whisper.

'If I let you go you'll fall on your backside.'

Good! It might knock some sense into her. His calmness infuriated her.

He smiled, a rueful twist of the lips. 'You are the most beautiful woman I have ever met, Cassie Campbell.' With that he pulled her shirt back over her still straining breasts, smoothed it down across her stomach and waist, and with one deft movement placed her on the other bench again. 'I'll give you a moment, shall I?'

He vaulted lightly out of the tree.

What was he doing? Her jaw dropped. He couldn't leave just like that.

He glanced up, his eyes twinkling. 'You've got to expect a few pins and needles, Cassie, when something has been asleep that long.'

With that he sauntered off, whistling.

CHAPTER EIGHT

SOL wheeled Alec up the ramp and into the foyer. He grinned at the kitten curled in Alec's lap. The nursing home would have to make an exception about pets today. It was Christmas.

And it wasn't anything like he'd expected.

Alec pointed. 'The dining room is at the end of that corridor.'

Anticipation surged through Sol as he headed towards the double doors. His footsteps seemed to echo Cassie's name. Heaven only knew what reaction he'd get when she saw him. Heaven only knew what reaction he deserved. Because there was no two ways about it. He'd lost his head this morning. Lost his head, lost his control and, hell, for all he knew lost his mind.

Oh, he'd meant to kiss her. You bet he'd meant to kiss her. He'd lain awake most of last night coming to that conclusion. He'd decided if he didn't get a sign today of all days, Christmas Day, then tomorrow he'd quietly pack his bags and leave.

He'd got his sign.

He paused outside the double doors. He hadn't meant to kiss her like that, though. But when he'd stared down into her face, with her soft curves all pressed up against him, ten years of anticipation, of frustration, of need, had risen up and taken over. Before he'd known it he had been kissing her like a man possessed.

'What are you waiting for, laddie?'

Girding my loins and preparing for battle. He didn't say the words out loud, though. He didn't want people getting the wrong idea and thinking him crazy. Maybe he was crazy?

Crazy for Cassie.

Alec glanced up. 'Does Cassie know we're coming?'

'Nope,' he said, and Alec chuckled.

The moment he pushed through the doors Sol's gaze settled on her. As if she were a magnet, a beacon. She wore a slinky red number that nipped in at the waist then dropped to swish around her calves. Need clenched through him; the air was punched out of his lungs. His knuckles whitened around the handles of Alec's wheelchair.

The desire he'd felt for her ten years ago hadn't abated. It hadn't died through lack of contact, through distance, as it should have done. It had grown. It didn't make sense.

Dammit, it didn't make any sense whatsoever. But what coursed through him when he stared at her threatened every shred of his control.

As if she sensed him there, she glanced up from where she bent over an elderly woman. Her eyes widened, and the little air he'd managed to get into his lungs slammed back out again. Everything around him receded. Sound and movement all faded into the background as she stared at him. It surged back when, unsmiling, she waved him to another table and turned away.

She couldn't have made it plainer if she'd tried.

What did you expect, Adams? Bells and whistles? You asked for a sign and you got one.

Yep. He had his sign. Cassie Campbell's defences were crumbling around her. He wheeled Alec to the table she'd indicated. This morning she'd come alive in his arms and it had been like nothing he'd ever experienced. He'd made up that much ground this morning and he intended to make up a hell of a lot more before the evening was over. His mouth stretched into a grim smile. This was one Christmas neither one of them would ever forget.

Omigod, Sol's here. Omigod, Sol's here.

The words pounded through Cassie's head until she thought she'd scream. Not content with stealing her peace of mind, he had to show up here too?

Hell—that was what today had been. Christmas lunch with the Parkers had been pure, unadulterated hell. A private hell of guilt and recrimination every single time she'd glanced into Jean's or Jack's face. The guilt worsened by the knowledge that they thought her quietness due to her supposed grief for Brian. Not shock because Sol had kissed her. Or because she'd kissed him back! After all, why would they think that? They'd never think her so faithless. It was only their second Christmas without Brian.

And it was her first Christmas—

She cut the thought off abruptly, almost savagely. What was Sol doing here? This party tonight was supposed to be her refuge, a balm to soothe frayed nerves and grief. He couldn't know how much she needed that tonight.

Out of the corner of her eye she watched him settle Alec then move towards her—a man on a mission.

If she was his mission he had another think coming.

'Sol.' She lifted her head with a smile as he drew near. 'Mrs Manetti, do you remember Sol Adams? He went to school with Brian and I, then left for the city.'

'Of course I do.' The older woman fixed Sol with her bright gaze. 'Sit yourself down, young man, and tell me what it was about the city that had you high-tailing it out of Schofield.'

'If you'll excuse me…'

With a bland smile and a sense of satisfaction Cassie moved away. Mrs Manetti was as sharp as a tack and claimed to remember every child who'd grown up in Schofield since the forties. If she could, she'd grill Sol for hours on what he'd done since he'd left town.

She wasn't stupid enough to think Mrs Manetti would achieve hours, but it was a hell of a man who'd get away in less than fifteen minutes. Sol might be a hell of a man, but he was stuck. Her spirits lifted. Needles and pins, huh? She'd give him needles and pins.

Her smile came easily as she made her way around the room, chatting, oohing and aahing over photographs of grandchildren and great-grandchildren. Every year the nursing home threw its doors open to the entire town. The older folk welcomed everyone to sit and chat whilst the younger generations helped in the kitchen. It made for a big, bustling party Cassie could lose herself in.

She kept one eye firmly fixed on Sol, though. As soon as she saw him start to extricate himself from Mrs Manetti she moved towards the kitchen. She wanted to time it right. Stand up now, Sol, she silently ordered.

He did. He glanced around. Found her.

Unhurried, she made for the door of the kitchen. Two steps before she reached it she felt the vital heat of his body behind her. One step. She turned with a smile, 'Sol.' She pushed into the kitchen. 'Look who's here to help, everyone!'

The entire Parker clan and ensemble cast turned. Tracey hurried forward. 'Just the man I need.' Without another word she dragged him to the far end of the kitchen.

Jack, at the sink, hunched his shoulders, then grunted a greeting as Sol and Tracey passed. Jean patted Cassie's cheek. 'That tray of *hors d'oeuvres* is ready, if you'd like to take it out.' Cassie seized it and swirled out of the kitchen again.

Hors d'oeuvres were followed by cold barbe-cued chicken and salad, and finished off with platters of watermelon and fruitcake. Cassie helped serve the feast, all the while avoiding Sol. She knew she couldn't put him off for ever, but there was a mischievous kind of satisfaction in thwarting him until she was ready.

Not that she'd ever be ready.

Don't be such a drama queen, she ordered. Sure, they'd lost their heads this morning, but it didn't mean she'd let it happen again. Ever. Because one thing had become very, very clear—one thing about this morning overshadowed everything else: Sol walking away, whistling. That was exactly what Sol would do when his holiday here was over. He'd walk away and he wouldn't look back. Just like ten years ago.

'How'd you like my trifle?' she asked Alec as she laid the last platter of fruitcake on his table and took the vacant seat beside him.

'It was real nice.'

'Good.' Reaching out, she scratched Rudolph's ears. He stretched in Alec's lap and started to purr. A bit like she had in Sol's lap this morning. With a grimace, she pulled her hand back.

'Can I give you some Christmas advice, Cassie?'

Alec only ever called her Cassie when he was serious. She didn't want serious. 'You mean advice about Christmas?'

'I mean advice *because* it's Christmas.'

Uh-huh—fabulous. She sat back. 'Okay, hit me with it.'

'It's no fun getting old, lass, and it's no fun dying alone.'

She opened her mouth to tell him he wasn't alone then closed it again. He meant alone as in not having a special person. Not having Pearl.

'I drove her away,' he said, as if reading her mind.

'And you never remarried.' She sighed.

'Don't go getting all sentimental on me, girl,' he warned. 'Pearl wasn't the love of my life.'

Cassie jerked back and stared.

'I never got involved with another woman because Pearl betrayed me.'

Betrayed him?

'And I made the decision to never trust another woman as long as I lived.'

Sadness swept through her. 'Oh, Alec, I'm sorry.'

He shook off her sympathy. 'I buried myself the day Pearl left, and it's the biggest mistake I ever made. Don't you go making the same mistake. Don't you go dying lonely.'

Cassie stared at him. She didn't know what to say.

'End of lecture,' he finished gruffly. 'Tell me you'll think about it.'

'I'll think about it.' She wouldn't be able to help it. She'd never seen her life so starkly presented before. But it was only one view of the picture, wasn't it? Confusion clamoured around her. 'Fruitcake?' She offered the platter around, then fled.

Stepping onto the lawn, Cassie hauled in a breath. Light spilled from the three sets of double glass doors in the dining room, and she carefully moved out of it and into the thicker darkness of the garden. Roses and gardenias drenched the air with their scent. Cicadas started up down by the river.

Alec was wrong. There were worse things than dying alone. She hugged herself. Besides, she wasn't cutting herself off. She was surrounded by family, by friends, and by people who cared for her. She was surrounded by love. Just not the kind of love he was talking about. No big deal.

A figure emerged from one of the doors. Sol.

She watched him for a moment, then expelled a long, slow breath. She'd made him wait. Now she simply wanted this conversation over.

'Over here,' she called when he peered out into the darkness.

He moved towards her. 'I saw you slip out.'

'Really? How surprising.'

'I'm not going to apologise about this morning.'

He stood so close she could feel his heat. She refused to tilt her head to look up at him, refused to give him anything he could interpret as an invitation. 'So you've already said.' She moved off to trace a path around the garden, hoping the scent of roses would drive the smell of Sol from her nostrils. She plucked a gardenia from the hedge and held it to her nose.

'So you've finally decided to stop avoiding me?'

She couldn't tell if he was angry or not. For a moment sadness squeezed the air out of her lungs. Once upon a time she would've known. All it had taken was one kiss to break down the bonds of a friendship she'd once held dear.

Her lips twisted. Actually, it had been a whole lot more than one kiss. Still…

'Cassie?'

'You walked in here tonight and just like a man you expected my undivided attention from the moment I saw you. Sorry to disappoint you, Sol, but there were a whole lot of other people higher on my list this evening than you.'

'Touché.'

She heard the smile in his voice and irritation surged up her backbone. 'One-upmanship has nothing to do with this.' This wasn't a game where you scored points. This was her life. 'You walk back into town and into my life and you think you can call all the shots.' Her hands went to her hips. 'Nobody calls the shots in my life anymore except me.' She was surprised to find herself breathing hard, as if she'd run a great distance.

'And Brian.'

It took several seconds for Sol's words to sink in. 'Brian?' She tried to laugh. It sounded shaky rather than defiant. 'Are you crazy?'

'If it wasn't for Brian you wouldn't lock yourself away from life the way you're doing.'

'I'm not—'

'If it wasn't for Brian you'd trust the people around you to support any decision you made to move on.'

A cold hand clamped over her heart. 'I do trust—'

'If it wasn't for Brian—' Sol clasped her chin in his fingers and forced her eyes to his '—you wouldn't keep punishing yourself like this.'

She chopped her forearm down on his in the darkness and broke his hold. 'For God's sake,' she hissed. 'It's Christmas.'

'It's time you stopped punishing yourself, Cassie. It's time you took a chance again. On loving a man. On having a family. The family of your dreams: a husband and babies. Babies who'll play with Fran's babies, and Tracey's.'

Her heart lodged in her throat. She wanted to run, but her feet were cemented to the ground.

'The argument you had with Brian the day he died was about having a baby, wasn't it?' He gave a harsh laugh. 'He didn't want to share you with anyone, not even a child, did he?'

Despair clamoured through her. She tried to stem the images that flooded her.

'And you're denying yourself the right to have a baby because you blame yourself for his death.'

She shook her head, fighting the urge to hide her face in her hands. 'Drop this, Sol.'

'No.'

No? Anger shot through her. 'What if I can't have a baby, Sol? What then?' In the darkness she could sense him reaching out for her. 'Don't touch me.' Even she was shocked by the coldness of her voice.

'I'll tell you one thing, Cassie. You're not half the woman I think you are if that's what you're hiding behind, if that's why you won't move forward. Because you're too scared to find out.'

Hiding? Move forward!

Something inside her snapped. Anger so thick she could taste it, so dark she could barely see through it, speared into her. She placed two hands in the middle of Sol's chest and pushed with all her might. He gave way before her.

'You think you have all the answers, Sol, but you don't know anything.' Her mouth twisted all out of shape. 'You don't know how I showed up in Emergency at three o'clock in the morning bloodied and bleeding. Do you have an answer for that?'

She pushed and he gave way.

'You don't know how I came in with a broken arm because Brian had thrown me down the back steps. You don't have an answer for that, do you?'

She heard his quick intake of breath and was glad. She pushed him again. He wasn't Sol any more, but a darker shape in the blackness that enclosed her. 'You don't know how I miscarried then and there.'

'Hell, Cassie.'

'What? No answer? This *is* what you wanted to hear, isn't it?' She pushed him back as he loomed closer, fiercely glad when he fell back before her. 'And you don't know the dreadful things I screamed at Brian the next morning. About how he'd killed our baby.' She gave a harsh laugh. 'The baby I gave to him in one breath then took away in the next. The baby he hadn't known about until that moment.' The baby he'd have done anything to protect if only he'd known she was pregnant. If only she'd told him sooner.

Nausea rose in her throat. She swallowed it back. 'And you don't know about the bungled curette or the infection, or how I almost died, and how it meant I couldn't make Brian's funeral, and how glad I was about that.'

Each sentence was punctuated with shoves in Sol's solid chest until it wasn't there to push against any more…and she had no strength left in her arms to push with anyway.

Breathing hard in the darkness, Cassie closed her eyes. When she opened them a sliver of moon appeared from behind a cloud. It didn't provide much light, but it was enough to see Sol half sprawled in a hedge in front of her.

Her jaw dropped. She'd pushed Sol into a hedge? She, who spouted off that she deplored violence, had pushed Sol into a hedge? As if he were the physical manifestation of the demons that plagued her dreams at night? Shame and despair fought inside her. She grabbed his arm and hauled him to his feet. She motioned to the hedge, then him. 'I'm sorry.'

'Cassie, I—'

'I don't want to talk about it.' She spun away.

'You can't lay that out there like that and then walk away.'

Oh, no? Just watch her. 'What are you going to do? Put a Band-Aid on it? Do you think you can make this right again?'

He lifted his hands and raked them through his hair. Her fingertips tingled. She knew how thick that hair was, how soft and springy.

He shook his head. 'There isn't a Band-Aid big enough for something like that.'

Exactly. 'Nobody else knows I was pregnant.' She sensed the question that hung in the silence between them. 'It seemed pointless to add that to their grief as well.' It would only have hurt them. 'I'd appreciate it if you didn't mention it to anyone.' He dragged a hand down his face, then nodded. With a sigh she turned to leave.

'Cassie?'

She stopped, but didn't turn around, her body bone-weary, as if it had just run and run and had finally stopped but knew the race wasn't over yet. Sol moved towards her until he stood directly behind her. The heat from his body mingled with hers, but he didn't touch her.

'I'm sorry about your baby, Cassie.'

His words flooded her with images she'd done her best to keep at bay all day. She wanted to cover her ears, but her arms had grown too heavy. She wanted to run, but her legs wouldn't move.

Your baby. The words pierced through her. *Her baby.* It should have been her first Christmas with *her baby.* She should be holding it in her arms and—

'Your baby deserves to be mourned, Cassie. It would've been beautiful and strong, just like you, and it deserved its chance at life.'

Her face crumpled in the dark as she fell to her knees. Her shoulders shook as sobs fought for release.

In one quick motion Sol swept Cassie up in his arms and carried her to a garden bench. Holding her close, he murmured meaningless words against her hair while she buried her face against his chest and sobbed.

He'd made her cry. She'd asked him to leave well enough alone and he'd paid no heed, so sure he knew better.

Idiot. He'd hurt Cassie. That was unforgivable.

A great gulf of sorrow opened up inside him when he thought of her baby. His eyes stung. She would've had a beautiful baby, and she'd have made a beautiful mother. More than anything he wished he could make it right.

Impossible. He should've left well enough alone. It was senseless to put her through this pain. He'd charged in, convinced he had all the answers. When he'd found the crack in her perfect life he'd pushed and pushed at it until she'd shattered. And he didn't have the answers to put her back together again.

What did he think he was doing? Laying the ghost of Brian to rest? Trying to fight the ghost because ten years ago he hadn't stayed to fight the man? His lips twisted in the dark. He deserved to be hung from the nearest tree and left for the crows.

He hadn't deserved to be chosen then and he didn't deserve it now.

Cassie's sobs eased to hiccups, but he didn't relax his hold. He held her close and rocked her, hoping he could provide a shred of comfort in the hell he'd forced her to relive. 'I'm sorry, Cassie. I'm sorry.' He said the words over and over as he rocked her.

The night blurred. Cassie had lost her baby.

In his arms, Cassie lifted her head. He heard her quick intake of breath. 'Sol, you're crying.'

Was he? The wind stirred, cooling the moisture on his cheeks. He lifted one helpless shoulder. 'Your baby, Cassie. I wish…'

Her eyes flooded with fresh tears. 'You're crying for my baby, Sol?'

He couldn't answer. Embarrassment ripped through him, then defiance.

She lifted a hand to his cheek, urging his eyes back to hers. 'Thank you,' she whispered.

He tucked her head back under his chin and leaned against the hard wooden bench, welcoming the pinch where it dug into his back. He couldn't logically explain his grief for her lost baby. All he knew was that he wanted to keep her here in his arms and never let anything hurt her again—to let her lie here and think about her baby, if that was what she wanted, without harm or hindrance.

But not alone. He didn't want her carrying a burden like that alone ever again.

It was a long time before either one of them spoke.

'I haven't cried for my baby since the day I yelled at Brian,' Cassie finally said.

The import of her words slowly soaked into him. He shifted so he could look down at her face. She stared back, unblinking. 'You haven't?'

'No.'

He gave her a little shake. 'You can't bottle stuff like that up, Cassie. It's bad for you.'

A smile peeped out. 'Don't you mean it's bad for you, because I push you into hedges and then soak the front of your shirt?'

'I've got broad shoulders.'

Her smile faded. 'So have I.'

'Yes, you have.' He had no intention of denying her strength. 'Make me a promise, Cassie. Promise me you'll never bottle up something that big again. I don't care where in the world I am, but get word to me and I'll come—okay?'

'You promise to come?'

'I promise to come.'

She glanced up at him, then down at her hands. 'I'm…umm…' She glanced up again. 'I'm glad it was you I cried with.'

Something frozen inside him started to melt.

'Now, don't go getting any notions about kissing me again—because that's not going to happen.'

She shifted as if she meant to move away, but he tightened his hold around her on the pretence of moving to a more comfortable position. The bench dug further into his back but he didn't care. 'No more kissing, huh?'

'No more kissing.' Her voice was firm.

He smothered a grin. 'I like kissing you, Cassie.'

'Sol!'

'Okay, okay.' He held up his hands. 'No more kissing… If you say so.'

'I say so.'

He wanted to kiss her. He had a feeling he'd always want to kiss her. But he was through with forcing his way on her. He had no right to think he knew better. If she said no kissing then, until she changed her mind—if she ever changed her mind—there'd be no kissing.

'And about bottling all that up.' Her hands twisted in her lap. 'It's not something I make a habit of, you know? It's just the people here who I love, who I could talk to about something like that, are Brian's family and friends.'

The very people she wanted to protect. Her heart was as big as it ever was—maybe bigger. In ten years Cassie hadn't changed much at all. 'Jean and Jack, Tracey and Fran, Keith and all the others love you for yourself, Cassie, not because you married Brian.'

'Of course.'

She said it too quickly. She didn't believe him. He sensed it at once. She'd never felt valued as a child, and as a teenager she'd been awestruck that Brian had chosen her. She'd never seen that Brian had been the lucky one.

Sol helped Alec to bed, then dragged himself through to the room he'd slept in as a boy. It contained nothing but his old single bed, Luke and Lew's double bunks, and an old chest of drawers. The walls were clean, almost Spartan.

He pulled his shirt over his head, then buried

his face in it. It still smelled of Cassie, sweet and intoxicating. He pulled himself up short, dropped it to the floor, then snapped open his jeans before his eyes lit on a neatly wrapped package on his bed. His Christmas present from Alec? He turned it over and over in his hands, then dropped to the side of the bed and un-wrapped it.

A photograph in a frame? He blinked. Then he stared. Alec, Pearl, Luke, Lew and himself all laughed out of that frame.

They laughed.

A card fell out and he read it.

I know you probably don't remember many happy times from your childhood, Sol. Just wanted to let you know there were a few and that I haven't forgotten them. Merry Xmas. Alec.

He stared at the photograph again. Alec's arm was around his shoulders. He would've been about twelve. They all looked so happy. Less than a year later Pearl had left, and it had all fallen apart.

She hadn't just left, though. She'd shattered Alec. She'd told him Sol wasn't his son. Sol dragged a hand down his face. He wished to God he'd known back then. At least it would've explained Alec's descent into alcoholism. His anger.

Yet for the first twelve and a half years of Sol's life it had been good. He stared at the photograph. Some days it had been great.

A family. He'd forgotten.

CHAPTER NINE

'HELLO?' Cassie sang through the back door.

'C'mon in, lass,' Alec called out. 'You're early.'

'Only half an hour. I've been painting all day and I've come to beg a glass of your lemonade.' She wiped the perspiration from her forehead. 'I swear it must be forty degrees in the shade out there.'

'Help yourself.' Alec motioned to the fridge and went back to the book open in his lap. His Christmas book. The one Sol had bought him.

Cassie glanced towards the living room door. She'd hoped her voice would drag Sol out of hiding. In fact she'd kept one ear cocked towards her back door all day, hoping he'd show up with banana sandwiches again.

To heck with sandwiches. She'd just wanted

him to show. He hadn't then and he didn't now. Disappointment sliced through her. She hadn't seen him since Christmas night. That was two whole days ago.

'Where's Sol?' When Alec slanted her a sly look she wished she hadn't asked.

'Out.'

She bit her tongue and didn't ask where. Or when he'd get back. 'Good book?'

'Very.' Alec didn't glance up.

Cassie shifted from one foot to the other. 'When does he go back to the city?'

'Dunno. Why?'

'No reason.' She poured a glass of lemonade. 'Would you like one?'

'Nope.'

She hovered for a moment, unsettled by the restlessness that surged through her. 'Do you mind if I take this out on the back veranda?'

'Nope.'

Sol hadn't arrived back by the time Cassie had cooked Alec's meal and finished off the few light chores she did for him, even though she stretched them out twice as long as usual. Not that she stretched them out on purpose. It was just so hot, that was all.

Sitting in her car, she felt that odd restlessness surge through her again. She wondered where Sol could be. She pushed the thought away. The Christmas sales were on. All the shops were trading late this evening. She could go and find herself a light summer read. She turned the engine over. Yeah, shopping sounded like a good idea. Who knew? She might even bump into Sol.

Two hours later, she decided shopping was the worst idea she'd had all year. Every person she'd ever known in her whole, entire life was shopping too. Everyone, that was, except Sol. And every single one of them asked her how he was doing. How was she to know? He was nothing to her other than a friend. A good friend.

Nothing more.

She collapsed into a chair at the coffee shop and ordered a cappuccino. 'No, make it a mu-guccino,' she amended. She wanted the biggest caffeine hit available. Weariness she had no right feeling at twenty-eight years of age crept through her, and she needed something to keep it at bay, to help her find the energy to drive home. She glanced at the shopping bag on the table in front of her. It hadn't been an entirely wasted trip.

'Cassie?'

A hand on her arm had her swinging in her seat to the table behind. Nessa. Her heart sank. Try as she might, she couldn't warm to the other girl. 'Hi, Nessa. Who's manning the Leagues Club tonight?'

Nessa tossed her long blonde hair over one shoulder. 'Cheryl.' She flicked her long red nails dismissively. 'I'm on holiday at the moment.'

'Lovely.' She tried to inject enthusiasm into her voice.

'How's Sol doing?'

Cassie blinked and made her face go blank. 'Sol Adams?' At Nessa's nod she said, 'Good, I guess. Alec hasn't said any different. I haven't seen Sol since...' she cocked her head to one side and pretended to contemplate it '...the nursing home do on Christmas night.'

'You haven't seen him?' Nessa darted a glance either side of her, then leaned in close. 'So there's nothing…' She waggled her hand in the space between them.

Cassie resisted the urge to roll her eyes. She leaned towards Nessa and waggled her hand back. 'Nothing…?'

'Between you and Sol?' Nessa whispered.

Cassie forced a laugh. 'Good Lord, no.'

Nessa's lips stretched into a cat-that-got-the-cream smile and all the fine hairs on the back of Cassie's neck lifted.

'Good.' Nessa gave a little girly shrug that set Cassie's teeth on edge. 'I wouldn't want to step on any toes.' She swept up her things and with a little wave left.

Wouldn't want to step on any toes? Cassie snorted. Nessa was the kind of girl who'd not only step on your toes but push you in the back and stomp down your entire length if she thought it meant getting what she wanted faster.

Dream on, sister. Cassie scowled. Sol wouldn't give a girl like you the time of day. Or would he? Her teeth ground together. Men could be alarmingly simple when it came to women.

'Whose eyes are you tearing out?'

Cassie blinked when Sol, as if stepping out of some fantasy inside her head, pulled out the chair opposite and sat down. He wore cream-coloured cargo shorts and a navy shirt and Cassie wanted to—

Oh, no, she didn't! He wasn't going to turn her inside out with that grin of his. No, sirree. She tried to look away but her eyes wouldn't obey, so she glared at him instead. 'Would you ever go out with a girl like Nessa?'

'Nessa?' He frowned. 'Nessa who?' A waitress appeared at his elbow with the speed of light. 'Hot chocolate,' he ordered, then glanced at Cassie. 'A big one like that.' He pointed to Cassie's mug.

He smiled that heart-stopping smile—only it wasn't directed at her, it was aimed at the waitress, who was in danger of melting into a puddle at his feet. Indignation kicked through her.

'Nessa?' he repeated.

'You know—the receptionist at the Leagues Club?'

'Oh, yeah, I remember her.'

He did, huh? She jabbed her spoon into the froth of her cappuccino. 'Well?'

'Why?'

'Because she was just in here and she gets right up my nose!'

'I'd never go out with anyone who got up your nose, Cassie.'

He said it with such straight-faced seriousness Cassie had to laugh. She knew he was joking, but her lethargy, her bone-crushing weariness fled, replace with a zest that sped through her veins.

He smiled as the waitress set his hot chocolate in front of him. 'Thanks.' Then he nodded to her package on the table. 'What did you get?'

'Books,' she mumbled. She wished she'd put the bag at her feet. Heat mounted high on her cheekbones.

He motioned towards it. 'May I?'

For the life of her she couldn't think of a single reason why he couldn't. She shrugged. 'Sure.'

He glanced into the bag and a grin spread from ear to ear. 'Georgette Heyer, huh? One, two…five Georgette Heyers? You never struck me as a Regency romance kind of girl.'

'Woman,' she corrected. 'And Georgette Heyer can sum up a character—' she snapped her fingers under his nose '—like that. She's great.'

'I don't doubt it.'

His grin grew. She folded her arms. 'What?'

'They're all about girls on the hunt for husbands. It doesn't strike me as your kind of thing.'

'Well, they all manage to find perfect husbands, don't they? I figure they're smarter than me. I might learn a thing or two.'

He leaned across the table and his scent hit her in the stomach. And lower. She wanted to open her mouth and taste him on her tongue. She couldn't look away.

'Does that mean you're reconsidering men and marriage?'

The darkness of his eyes seemed to draw the darkness out of her very soul. He made her want things she could never have. Like him. She wanted him. Badly. But marriage?

She shot back in her seat. 'No way.' Not in this lifetime.

'Cassie.' He laid his hand over hers. 'I—'

'They're just a bit of fun, Sol. Fairytales.' She

removed her hand, seized the bag of books and dropped them to her feet.

He stared at her for a long moment. Then he reached into his pocket and pulled out something. He turned it over and over in his hands, then laid it on the table in front of her. 'This was my Christmas present from Alec.'

She glanced into his face. Coffee shop noises rattled around them. Her hand trembled when she reached out to pick it up. She glanced at it and her heart lurched. A photograph of Sol and his family. They all looked so happy, so perfect.

'This is what we should all strive for, Cassie. A happy, loving family.'

Confusion fumbled through her. 'But it fell apart.'

'It doesn't matter. For the greater part of my childhood I was part of a happy family.' His eyes bored into hers. 'I know you never knew your father. And I know your marriage to Brian was unhappy. But still—' he nodded at the photograph '—it is possible to achieve that.'

For some, maybe. She stared at the photograph and sadness shuffled through her. Why hadn't this happiness lasted for them? She ran her fingertips across their faces. 'I wonder why it all went wrong?'

'Because Pearl told Alec he wasn't my real father.'

Cassie gaped at him. 'She what?'

Pearl betrayed me.

She stared at Sol, aghast. 'Is it true?'

'Yep.'

'Did you know?'

'I didn't find out until I turned eighteen.'

It all started to make awful sense. She closed her eyes.

'And yet as a family we could've overcome that.'

Her eyes flew open. 'You reckon?' She couldn't see how any family could overcome something like that.

'We went our own ways. We pulled apart instead of together. If we'd pulled together we would've made it.'

He really believed that? She wished she shared his optimism. She handed him back the photograph.

'You don't believe me?'

She shrugged. She didn't want to tarnish a conviction he held dear.

He put the photo back in his pocket. 'Then I'll have to prove it to you.' He reached out and brushed a finger across her cheek. 'You'll see.'

Then he was gone.

Three days. Another three days had passed and she hadn't clapped eyes on Sol once. Hadn't even caught a glimpse of him in the distance.

Not that she cared. She didn't miss his grin, didn't miss his laughter, and she sure as hell didn't miss the challenges he tossed at her when she least expected it.

She missed ogling those shoulders, though.

Nonsense! She slapped Alec's plate down in front of him.

'What's eating you, girlie?' he complained.

'Nothing,' she snapped. He always called her girlie when he wanted to get a rise out of her.

'Nothing a husband and babies wouldn't fix,' he muttered.

Her jaw dropped. Her mouth opened and closed. 'Of all the chauvinistic—'

She couldn't think of words bad enough to describe it. She threw the teatowel to the table and flounced out through the door. 'You can do your own dishes,' she tossed over her shoulder.

But his laughter followed her all the way down the drive and out to her car.

She didn't need a husband. She already had everything she needed, thank you very much, and eventually the people around here would realise that and leave her alone. Before Sol had showed up they had all known.

It was all Sol's fault.

Even in the midst of her anger she realised it was hardly a fair accusation. Still, thank heavens it was Thursday night. Family night. There was nothing like family night to bolster her resolve, to remind her of everything she could still lose.

She'd lost Brian and she'd lost his baby. She wasn't losing his family.

Her temper hadn't improved when, less than ten minutes, later she stomped up the path leading to her front door.

'Hey, Cassie.'

She started violently, clutched her heart, then

staggered to the wooden bench that ran under the front window. 'Lord, Tracey—you startled the beejeebies out of me.'

Tracey grinned. 'I haven't seen anybody jump that high since the last *Nightmare on Elm Street* movie, and I was just a kid back then.'

'I was a million miles away.'

'You looked fit to slice someone up for supper.'

'Just Alec being his usual cantankerous self is all. But c'mon in.' She jumped up and led the way through to the cool of the kitchen. 'What's up?'

Her head shot round at Tracey's hesitation. Tracey didn't hesitate over anything. Silently, she handed her a can of cola, then motioned her to a seat at the table.

'I wanted to show you something.'

'Okay.' She popped her own can of soda and took a sip.

'You know how I've always been mad keen on photography?'

'Uh-huh.'

'Well, I've always been mad keen on photos too.'

'Okay.' Seemed logical so far. 'And?'

Tracey made an impatient noise in the back of her throat. 'Here—see for yourself.' She shoved a packet of photos into Cassie's hand. 'They say a picture's worth a thousand words.'

Cassie glanced at the top photograph and her jaw dropped. It didn't need a thousand words. One would do.

Sol!

She riffled through the rest of the photographs anyway. She didn't get it. These photos had to be at least thirty years old. They couldn't be Sol. 'Where did you get these?'

Tracey bit her lip. 'From our family albums. That's Dad on his twenty-fifth birthday.'

Her stomach turned to stone. Jack? She stared at the top photo again. Then that meant…

'You see it too?'

It wasn't really a question, but Cassie nodded anyway.

'What do you think we should do?'

She had no idea. But through her confusion one fact clarified itself in her brain with horrifying precision. The evidence she held in her hand could blow the Parker family apart. She handed the photos back to Tracey. 'Have you spoken to anybody about these?'

'No.'

'You could always burn them.'

'I thought about that, but it didn't seem right somehow.'

Cassie thought back to the fifteen-year-old boy who'd sat in a tree and held her hand. Her heart clenched. No, it didn't seem right. She dragged her hands down her face. 'Would you like me to talk to Sol?'

'Would you?' Tracey seized her hand, her smile a mixture of relief and eagerness. 'It's what I was hoping you'd say.'

What a mess. She gripped the bridge of her nose between thumb and forefinger. Did Jack and Jean know? It could explain their reactions the night she'd brought Sol round for drinks. Yet they'd done nothing, said nothing.

'When did you first guess?'

'There was something about Sol I couldn't put my finger on the night of the dinner party. Afterwards I hunted out the photo albums. Funny, isn't it? If he'd stayed in Schofield I probably would never have noticed the similarity.'

Did Sol know? Her heart clenched. Did he even want to know? She gripped Tracey's hand. 'What are you hoping for out of all this?'

'I don't really know,' she confessed. 'I just don't think something this big should be kept a secret.'

Cassie stared at the packet of photos clutched in Tracey's hand.

'And you know what else, Cassie?' Tracey's chin lifted. 'I like the idea of having another brother. I like it a lot.'

Tracey wanted it all. She wanted them to be one big happy family. Heck. They needed a miracle.

Cassie hoisted herself into the tree house. Three magpies warbled in the early-morning sun. Down towards the river heat shimmered in the air already. For about the fiftieth time that morning she wondered at the wisdom of asking Sol to meet her here.

Especially after what had happened last time.

She pushed the thought away. She needed

somewhere private, where they wouldn't be disturbed. That left the tree house or the cemetery. And she and Sol had always met in this tree. She glanced at her watch. Maybe he hadn't got her message. She went to twist her wedding band round and round her finger, then remembered she'd taken it off last night and forgotten to put it back on this morning.

The screen door slammed. Cassie's stomach tightened and she gripped her hands in front of her. She couldn't hear his footfalls on the soft grass, but she imagined him moving closer and closer until he stood beneath her. A bolt of something fierce and sweet shook her when she saw him.

He grinned up at her through the branches. 'You could've asked me to meet you anywhere, Cassie, but I've gotta admit a secret rendezvous in a tree house adds a certain flavour.'

Yep, major mistake meeting here. The kisses they'd shared hung heavily in the air, making Cassie's limbs languid with longing, tempting her to take right up where they'd left off last time and to hell with the consequences.

She couldn't help noticing the way his arm muscles bulged as he hoisted himself into the tree, or the tanned length of his legs as he sat on the bench at right angles to her. His height and breadth dominated the space. His scent drifted across to her, dominating her senses. Maybe it'd be a whole lot easier dealing with Sol if he didn't look so good all the time.

It'd help if she could remember how to breathe too.

Everything she found most attractive in a man came together in Sol—his height, the breadth of those shoulders, with their arms strong enough to scoop you up and hold you near, the dark thickness of his hair her fingers constantly itched to touch, the long lean length of his legs. Not to mention his crooked smile, those deep brown eyes, and…just everything. How was a woman supposed to keep her mind and her wits about her when she was dealing with her dream lover?

Good grief! Not lover. Dream…uh…*boat*. Yeah, that was what she meant.

Get a grip, she ordered herself. She went to slap herself upside the head, but realised how ridiculous that would look so stared down towards the river instead. She couldn't see the river itself, only the line of trees that marched along its banks. She forced herself to imagine the slow moving waters until her pulse-rate approached something akin to normal. Only then did she turn back to Sol.

She found him watching her steadily. Her shoulders suddenly sagged and she threw her hands in the air. 'I don't even know where to start.'

He gave her that slow, crooked grin. The breath hitched in her throat. 'Would it help if I kissed you?'

Her pulse rate skyrocketed. 'No!' He was only teasing. She knew that. Still… She pointed her finger at him. 'No kissing.'

He seized the finger, brought it to his lips and pressed a kiss to its very tip. 'Spoilsport.' Then he released it.

She clasped it in her lap, where it throbbed and tingled. He grinned as he leant back and stretched his arms along the back of the bench, his legs relaxed in front of him, his whole posture an invitation to her to take up the position she'd assumed when they were last together in the tree house—straddled in his lap.

She'd never been more tempted by anything in her life.

'What about this girl back in Sydney you're thinking of marrying?' she suddenly accused him.

Sol went very still. Although his posture didn't change, Cassie sensed the tension that shot through him. He gazed at her, long and hard, and something shifted inside her.

'I'm not currently in a relationship, Cassie.'

He wasn't? Something suspiciously like hope flared to life inside her. She tried to quell it. Tried and failed.

'There's no girl in the city that I'm hoping to marry.'

There was no girl? There was no engagement? Then who—?

The craziest notion she'd ever had hit her right between the eyes.

His grin, when it came, was slow and knowing. 'So…'

Cassie swallowed. Her heart hammered against

her ribs. 'So?' She didn't know if it was his grin, the promise in his voice, or the plan solidifying in her brain.

'So I'm all yours, Cassie.' His body mirrored his open invitation.

This plan… It was perfect. She could keep everyone together. Happy families.

It would solve everything!

The grin he sent her was pure wickedness. 'If you want me, that is.' His grin told her he knew she wanted him.

Her mouth watered. For a moment all she could do was feast her eyes on him. 'Oh, I want you, Sol.' Her words drove out any semblance of relaxation from his posture. 'But I'm an old-fashioned kind of girl.'

His arms no longer stretched out along the bench. His legs no longer stretched out in front of him. He leaned forward, elbows on knees, eyes intent on her face. She met them steadily. 'I want you, I want to have babies, and I still think you're the best friend I've ever had.' His eyes dropped to the third finger of her left hand and she suddenly felt naked.

'And?' The word was ragged, almost harsh.

She lifted her chin. 'Would you marry me, Sol?'

The words had hardly left her lips before Sol surged to his feet, dragging her with him. His mouth crushed down on hers. Cassie clung to him as the world spun.

She blinked when he lifted her head. 'You're mine, Cassie Campbell.' His eyes glittered. 'And make no mistake. I won't be satisfied with anything less than all of you.'

His words were low, but fierce. Fear skittered up her spine. What was she doing? She must be crazy to think she—

His hands on her face gentled, as if he sensed her fear. 'I will never hurt you, Cassie. I swear.'

His eyes urged her to believe him. She stared back, mute, trapped by a web of emotions she was powerless to unravel.

'I will never raise so much as a finger to you.'

His fingers stroked her face. Her blood pumped beneath his fingertips.

'I don't care if we fight with as much intensity as we make love.'

A tremble shook her.

'I don't care if you hit out at me, throw things at me, or scream things that can tear out a man's heart.' His hands tightened on her face. 'I will *never* raise my hand to you.' His eyes refused to release hers. 'Okay?'

She stared back. She believed him. She didn't know how or why, but every fibre of her being told her he would never harm her physically. She moistened her lips, then nodded. His mouth came back down on hers. Hard. And she knew it was a claim. He was claiming her as his. It answered something primitive deep inside her, because at the same time he was telling her he was hers. All hers. And she wanted him with a fierceness that matched his hunger.

They were both breathing hard when he lifted his head. 'I know you're an old-fashioned girl, Cassie.'

She nodded, barely able to hear him over the pounding in her ears.

'So this is going to be a short engagement. Very short.'

She stared up at him, mesmerised. He grinned that wicked grin, and his lips lowered to hers

with an agonising slowness that had her sus-
pended between two breaths. His teeth tugged
gently at her lower lip. A tremble shot from the
top of her head down to the soles of her feet.

'How about this afternoon?'

His tongue grazed the sensitive flesh of her
inner lips. Desire shot through her so thick and
fast it rocked her.

'Today is a good day to get married.'

His lips trailed a path of fire to her ear. His
tongue plunged in and then out suggestively. He
did it again. A moan whispered from her. He
chuckled against her throat as she sagged against
him, her knees barely holding her up. His arm
tightened around her waist and he took her with
him as he moved back and down, until he was
seated on the bench and she was straddled in his
lap…just as she'd pictured earlier.

'I don't think you want a long engagement
either.' He moved against her, making her aware
of his desire. 'Do you?'

Her hands tightened convulsively on his
shoulders as sensation swamped her. 'But it
can't be today.'

'No?'

He trailed a fingertip along her collarbone—a trail of fire he followed with his tongue. Sol, stop it,' she almost sobbed, but she couldn't stop herself from arching against him. 'I can't think when you do that.'

'I don't want you thinking, Cassie. I want you naked and breathing hard.'

She stared at the mouth that uttered such tempting words and fell into it.

She surfaced to hear him say, 'Tomorrow, then. Marry me tomorrow, Cassie.'

No, no. Things were moving too fast. 'Stop it, Sol. Be serious. I want to talk to you.'

His eyes darkened as they roved across her face. 'I've never been more serious about anything in my life.'

'Then behave and let me talk.'

'What about tomorrow?' he persisted, his smile daring her to say yes.

'Too soon.'

'The day after, then?'

She had to grin. 'I'll think about it.'

'What did you want to talk about?' His fingers

fanned out around her throat, lightly stroking her flesh, slowly moving across her shoulders, dipping into the hollow of her collarbone, then lower.

'Sol,' she warned him, hardly able to breathe under his light, lazy touch.

'I'm only touching safe areas, Cassie.'

Safe! His fingers didn't stop.

'Does this feel safe?' She raked her finger-nails down his arms and he emitted a low growl.

'That's playing with fire.'

She nodded. 'We're in a tree house, Sol.' She hugged her arms around herself. 'And I want to wait until…'

'Until we're married,' he finished for her. His fingers stopped their exploration. He closed his eyes and dragged in a deep breath. They flew open again in the next instant and he speared her with them. 'I swear you're never going to forget the first time we make love.'

Anticipation surged through her. She lifted her chin and stared right back at him. 'Neither will you.'

He chuckled, a low, warm sound that vibrated

through her. 'This marriage is going to be one hell of an experience. Now, what did you want to talk about?' His eyes narrowed. 'Don't you go trying to put any conditions on this marriage, because I won't accept them.'

'They're not conditions.' Her hands convulsively rubbed the tops of her arms as she eyed him nervously. Marriages shouldn't contain conditions, and she wanted this to be a real marriage.

His eyes gentled. He took her hands in his own. 'What did you want to talk about?'

Her eyes dropped from his. He ducked his head so he could see into her face. Her hands tightened in his. 'Oh, Sol, Schofield is my home.'

'And you'd like to stay here?'

She hesitated, then nodded. He stared at her steadily. 'We can do that. Most of my work can be done remotely.'

'It can?' A load lifted from her shoulders and excitement curled its way up her spine. 'We can?'

He grinned. 'Sure we can. But I will need to

spend a few days each month in Sydney, and I'd like you to accompany me.' She nodded eagerly. 'I won't live in that house you and Brian shared.'

Good grief, no. The idea was hideous. A shy hope filtered through her. 'What about my house?' She nodded over the fence.

'You'd share that with me?'

She swallowed, then nodded. 'I'd like to spend our honeymoon night there.' She felt the blush blossom across her cheeks. 'And it means we could, uh, keep an eye on Alec.'

'It does.' Sol's eyes darkened until they were almost black. 'The day after tomorrow, Cassie. The sooner you marry me the—' He broke off, as if catching himself. He pulled in a breath. 'Is it important for you to be married in a church?'

'No.' She twisted her hands together. 'But I would like our families there. I'd want the Parkers and Alec there. That's important to me.'

He gave a curt nod.

'And Sol?'

'What?'

'We can't get married the day after tomorrow.'

His brows drew down low over his eyes. 'Why

not? Hell, Cassie, I…' He dragged a hand down his face. 'How long do you want me to wait?'

'A month.'

'A month!'

His impatience did strange things to her stomach. 'We need to give a month's notice before we can marry. It's the law.'

'A whole month?' Sol groaned. 'That'll try my patience like nothing else.'

'Which is why I'm going to remove myself from your presence.' She clambered out of his lap. 'I've a million things to do.' She darted a nervous glance at him. 'And stuff.'

'Stuff, huh?'

He rose, and she edged towards the ladder that led down into her yard. He leaned over and brushed his lips across hers, then vaulted out of the tree and strode away, whistling.

Cassie had to wait two whole minutes before her knees were steady enough for her to negotiate the ladder.

CHAPTER TEN

EXHILARATION gripped Sol, and a fierce posses-
siveness that frightened him with its intensity.
He was possessed by Cassie, intoxicated. He
wanted to turn back, find her, and lose himself
in her fragrant freshness, in the velvet of her
arms, in the scope of her smile.

He kept walking. *I'm an old-fashioned girl,*
kept ringing in his ears. She wanted to wait. And
he wanted what she wanted.

She wanted to marry him!

He leapt up and punched an arm in the air.
'Yes!' He didn't care if anyone saw him.

He kept walking.

And walking.

He stopped dead when he realised where his
steps had taken him. He hesitated. The back door
stood open...

Jean answered the back door at his knock.

'Sol! Come in.' She pushed the screen door open, kissed him on the cheek. 'Jack's in the shower, but he shouldn't be too long. Sit, sit.' She poured him a coffee.

'Thanks.' He sat and glanced around the kitchen. It was nice, homey. No wonder Cassie loved it. She'd brought some of that hominess into Alec's kitchen.

Jean smiled at him. No rancour showed in her face, no bitterness. 'You're up and about early today.'

He nodded. All that walking hadn't diminished his pent-up energy. It took all his effort not to fidget. He gritted his teeth. It was just as well he'd kept walking or he'd have climbed straight back up that tree and convinced Cassie they might have to wait a month for their wedding day, but it didn't mean they had to wait a month for their wedding night.

Everything inside him tensed at the thought. He set down his mug before he crushed it, and tried to think of something else. 'I...' For the first time he noticed Jean's attire—town dress, was what his mother had used to call it. 'You're up early too.' He started to rise. 'I didn't mean to interrupt—'

'Nonsense, Sol, sit down. You're family. It's my morning at the charity shop, that's all. I like to get in early and go over the accounts.'

Sol leaned back and admiration raked through him. 'You're a remarkable woman, Jean Parker.'

'Thank you, Sol. That's a lovely thing to say.' She buttered two slices of toast, slid two fried eggs on top and set them in front of him.

'I didn't mean for you to feed me!'

'Hush up and eat.'

He didn't pick up his knife and fork. He continued to survey Jean instead. 'Aren't you the least bit resentful? Don't you wish I'd stayed away?'

'Why would I want that?' She glanced up from where she buttered more toast. 'You're an innocent party in all this.'

'Aren't you livid with Jack?' If he'd been married to Cassie for thirty-two years and then found out she'd been unfaithful to him twenty-nine years ago… Time wouldn't dim that hurt.

Jack and Jean had accepted him with remarkable grace when he'd shown up on their doorstep two days before and told them what Alec had roared at him ten years ago—that Sol was Jack's son. Neither one of them had seemed all that surprised.

Jean pulled out the seat opposite and sat. 'I promised to love Jack in sickness and in health; in good times and in bad.' She sighed, her smile wistful. 'In every life there's always some bad along with the good, and love without forgiveness isn't really love at all.'

But Jack had cheated on her! 'I don't know how I'd—'

He broke off. He'd forgive Cassie anything. The realisation revealed the stream of vulnerability running right through the centre of his soul. He passed a hand across his eyes and nodded. 'You're right.'

Jean patted his hand. 'Eat up.'

He suddenly realised he was ravenous. 'Mmm…this is good.' And Cassie had asked him to marry her! Life was good. Life was very, very good.

Jean watched him. A smile hovered on her lips. She didn't speak again until he'd finished. 'Sol, I don't want you to think badly of Jack. If I can forgive him then so can you. He's a good man. He was my rock when Brian died.'

Sol met her gaze.

'And it all seems so long ago now,' she sighed. She clasped her hands together on the table in front of her. 'I'd not long had Fran. I was completely rapt in motherhood, to the exclusion of everything and everyone… including Jack. And Jack, being a man—men in those days thought they were sissies if they complained about feeling lonely or neglected—didn't say anything.' She stared at the wall opposite, a faraway look in her eyes. 'And Pearl had a way with the men.'

She snapped to suddenly. 'Oh, Sol, I'm sorry. I had no right to say such a thing.'

'Don't apologise for speaking the truth.' He sent her a wry smile. 'She'd have taken it as a compliment.'

Jean laughed. He liked the sound. 'So…' He hesitated. 'You knew? All those years ago?'

'Oh, yes. I locked Jack out of the house when I found out about him and Pearl. He spent the night on the veranda. I've never seen him so frightened of anything as he was when he thought he'd lose me and the baby. But I didn't know you were Jack's son.'

She suddenly reached across the table and touched his hand. 'He never regretted anything more than betraying me, but he doesn't regret you, Sol. The thought that you might've been his son tormented him.'

'But Pearl told him I was Alec's?'

'Yes.' Jean sat back. 'So we watched you grow up from a distance…and we always wondered. I even asked her myself once, but she told me the same thing.'

Sol gazed at her, shook his head. 'Didn't I say you were a remarkable woman?'

'Of course she is.' Jack came into the room, clapped Sol awkwardly on the shoulder. 'Morning, son.' He pressed a kiss to the top of Jean's head.

'Ooh, look at the time.' Jean leapt up. 'That's what I get for sitting around and gasbagging.'

But the smile she sent Sol was kind. She popped toast into the toaster.

'Don't fuss, woman,' Jack ordered. 'I'll take care of that. You're going to be late.'

'If you're sure?'

'Of course I'm sure.'

Jean kissed him. 'Bye, love.' And, with a wave to Sol, she left.

Jack rubbed his hands together. 'This is the one morning of the week when I have fried bread,' he confided with a grin. 'Do you want some?'

Cassie staggered up the steps, sagged against the back door and glanced at her watch. It wasn't even eight o'clock! Still so early.

Too early to visit Jack. Jean wouldn't have left yet.

Way too early to have turned her whole life on its head.

She fell through the door and collapsed into a chair. The house still smelled of paint. Had she really just asked Sol to marry her? She gripped the skin of her left forearm between thumb and finger and twisted hard.

Ouch!

Coffee. She needed coffee. Right now. This very instant.

She clicked on the kettle, doled a generous spoonful of coffee into a mug, then paced the length of the kitchen waiting for the water to boil.

One month and then she'd be married to Sol. Excitement trickled all the way down to her toes and curled them. She gazed out through the back door and across to Alec's yard. Proposing to Sol was just about the craziest thing she'd ever done.

Not *just about,* a tart voice in her head said. *It's absolutely the craziest thing.*

She grinned and hugged herself. Then the grin faded. Sol wanted her. It didn't take a rocket scientist to figure that one out. And he'd wanted her for a long time. But would it be enough?

For what?

She didn't know the question she was trying to ask, let alone the answer. She gave up trying to figure it out as the kettle came to the boil.

She drank her coffee like a drunk trying desperately to get sober. She'd watched her mother do it often enough. It hadn't worked then and it

didn't work now. Sol flooded her senses, intoxicated them. The desire he'd awoken in her clamoured along every nerve-ending, clawed at her
stomach. Images, raw and explicit, tormented
her as they played over and over in her mind,
refusing to let her settle. Her body wanted Sol,
it wanted release, and it wanted it now.

Man, oh, man, it was going to be a long month.
She made another coffee, sat at the table and
stared at the wall. Then, as if in a dream, she
stood, walked through the house, down the hall
and pushed open the door to the master bedroom.

A physical representation of what Sol had
awoken in her gleamed back its promise. Her
breathing grew shallow. They'd spend their honeymoon night here. She wondered what time
they'd get married. She wondered how long after
the ceremony it would be before they could
make it back here.

She slammed the door shut and fled down the
hall, back into the kitchen. She flopped into her
chair and wrapped her hands around her coffee
cup. Think of something else, she ordered.
Anything else. But she couldn't. Her mind

filled with Sol as she remembered the taste of him, the feel of him. She glanced up at the wall clock. She had to get out of here. Now. Before she called Sol and—

She leapt up. Early or not, she had to see Jack. Jean should've left by now.

It was eight-thirty when she pulled into their drive. Instead of going around the back and letting herself in, as she normally did, she pressed a finger to the front doorbell and waited.

Everything was about to change. Everything. Fear slid through her, but her love for the Parkers kept her from racing back to the car and speeding away. She had to do this. She crossed her fingers behind her back and prayed that she could make everything right.

Jack answered the door. 'Cassie.'

She could smell the fresh pine scent of his aftershave, and for a moment nerves almost overwhelmed her as she realised the enormity of what she was about to do, of everything she could lose. 'I, umm, need to speak to you.'

He cast a glance behind him. 'I...uh...it's very early.'

'Please?' If he put her off… 'It's important.'

She didn't need to say any more. Jack ushered her inside at once. For some reason the familiarity of the living room almost broke Cassie's heart.

'Cassie?'

She swung back to Jack. To her horror, she could feel her eyes fill.

'Cassandra, I should tell you—'

'No!' Panic pounded through her. 'Please let me speak first, because if I don't I'll—' Chicken out? No, she couldn't do that. She leapt forward, caught one of his hands in both her own. 'You know I love you, don't you, Jack?'

'Of course I do, Cassie.' He led her to the sofa, made her sit, patted her hand. 'What's all this about?'

'I don't just love you. I love you like I would a father.'

His face gentled. 'And I love you as if you were one of my own daughters.'

She clung to his words. She couldn't believe she was going to do this. 'Jack—' She gulped in a breath. 'I know you're Sol's real father.'

Jack's head reared back, then he groaned. He

dropped his elbows to his knees and his head to his hands. 'Oh, Cassie, what must you think of me?'

She touched his arm, wishing he'd look at her. 'Jack, I love you as much as ever. I still respect you as much as I ever did. I'm not here to judge you.'

He lifted his face and Cassie managed a smile for him. 'Do you know that the happiest day of my life was when you and Jean welcomed me into your family?'

'We were lucky to have you.'

She shook her head. 'Sol is a good man, Jack. He deserves all this too.'

Jack sat back and stared.

'You have to accept him into the family.' She rushed in quickly when he opened his mouth to speak. 'I know that it won't be easy telling Jean, but I'll do whatever I can to make the transition easier.' She bit her little finger. 'Jean will be hurt. I can't see any way around that. But Jack,' she gripped his hand, 'when she gets to know him she'll love Sol like she loves me, and maybe that'll make up for—'

The front door burst open and Jean hurried in.

'I forgot that recipe I promised Marjorie weeks ago, and she'll have my head if—' She pulled up short. 'Cassie!'

'She knows,' Jack said. 'She knows Sol is my son.'

Concern speared across Jean's face and Cassie's jaw dropped. 'You knew too?'

'Yes, dear.' Jean lowered herself to the sofa beside her and patted her hand. 'Are you okay?'

'Me?' she gaped. 'What about you? I mean—'

'I've had a long time to get used to the idea.' Jean reached across and tapped Cassie's jaw shut. 'Now, dear, when do you think we should tell everyone? Before or after Fran has her baby?'

'Oh, I—' A strange laugh wobbled out of Cassie. 'You'd better make it before. Tracey has caught on.'

'Oh, dear. Well, that settles it.'

'And while you're at it you might want to announce my engagement.' She stared from Jean to Jack and back again. 'I'm going to marry him. I'm going to marry Sol.'

* * *

From the kitchen, Sol listened to Cassie's words in stunned amazement. She was magnificent—an avenging angel. Everything that meant something to her in this life was on the line—or at least she'd thought it was.

And she'd done it all for him?

Nobody had done anything like that for him before. Ever. Hope surged through him in thick, hot waves. It had to mean she—

'Cassandra.' Jack pulled in a breath. 'I think we should tell you—'

Sol snapped to attention, shot his upper body round the kitchen doorway and shook his head wildly. He didn't want Jack giving him away—not now. Jack met his eyes, held them for the bricfcst of moments, then nodded. Satisfied, Sol moved back out of sight.

'Tell me what?' Cassie asked.

Sol held his breath, wondering if the older man would change his mind. He knew how much Jack loved Cassie.

'Have you spoken to Sol about this?'

Sol's shoulders sagged in relief. He heard the

grin in Cassie's voice when she said, 'He knows I plan to marry him.'

Jack didn't laugh. 'I meant have you spoken to him about his paternity?'

'No.'

She paused, and Sol had to fight the temptation to peer around the door again and drink in his fill of her. He ached for her, longed to go to her and put his arms around her and tell her this wasn't necessary. She didn't need to go into battle for him.

But part of him loved it that she did. He loved that she fought for what she believed in. But most of all he wanted her to see that this vision she had of them all becoming a whole and happy family was possible.

And he wanted her to realise that on her own. Without his interference. That and that alone kept him silent in the kitchen.

'Do you love him, Cassie?' Jean asked. 'Do you love Sol?'

Cassie hesitated. Sol waited and waited. Then it hit him—and the bottom fell out of his world.

'He's my best friend,' she finally said.

He rested his forehead against the cold metal

of the fridge, pulled in a breath, then let himself out through the back door. She hadn't asked him to marry her because he'd made her come alive. She'd asked him to marry her to keep the Parker family together. She wasn't an avenging angel but a sacrificial lamb. Bile rose in his throat as he strode out of the yard and stalked down the street.

Do you love him? Jean's question and Cassie's hesitation tormented him. He should've left the moment she'd arrived, but she'd jumped in so fast it had mesmerised him. *She* had mesmerised him.

What was that saying about eavesdroppers? He dragged his hands down his face. Whatever it was, he had a feeling he'd just proved it.

She had put everything on the line, though, and it could've backfired on her. She could've lost the lot.

The lot? His mouth twisted. She still thought she'd gained it by default, by marrying Brian. He slowed to a halt and rested his hands on his knees, like a jogger fighting for breath. He couldn't marry her. Not now. But there was something else he could give her. A gift that might make it possible for Cassie to finally move on and live her life to the full as she should.

'Happy New Year, Sol.'

Cassie smiled up at him, her eyes shining, and Sol couldn't help it. He leaned down and kissed her. One last time. 'Happy New Year, Cassie.'

The noise of the party spilled from the house. Sol knew he'd have to return soon. He'd slipped away for a moment to catch his breath, to strengthen his resolve, to remind himself what he had to do.

'Are you okay?'

No. He wanted to take her by the shoulders and shake her, howl a denial into the night. He didn't. It wasn't what she meant anyway. She was referring to Jack's announcement.

Two hours ago Jack had called everyone into the living room—a tight squeeze, considering almost half the town was there tonight—and announced that Sol was his son. And that he was proud to call such a man his son.

Jean had stood by Jack's side. She'd kissed Sol's cheek and smiled fiercely at everyone, daring their disapproval. Alec had sat nearby in his wheelchair, daring the same. Fran, Tracey and Cassie—always Cassie—had flanked them, their delight and their pride in Sol a tacit endorsement. In that moment Sol had glimpsed what it was Cassie treasured so dearly. What she'd been prepared to sacrifice.

She touched his arm and he came to. 'It's all good, Cassie. This is what I came home for.'

'You've been mobbed since the announcement. I haven't been able to get near you.' She started to edge away. 'I understand if you want some time alone.'

'No.' He captured her wrist, and the confusion in her eyes deepened. He knew his reserve puzzled her. Gritting his teeth, he led her into the deeper shadows of the backyard. Under his fingers her pulse leapt, and his heart clenched.

'I thought Jack was going to announce our engagement tonight too.'

Her voice was breathy, and he wished he were dragging her into the darkness for the reasons she obviously thought. He let go of her hand. 'I asked him not to.'

'Why?' The word dropped out of her.

His mouth pulled into a thin line. 'I'm sorry, Cassie, but I'm not going to marry you.'

She blinked, then took a half-step away. 'Why not?'

'Because the reason you asked me to marry you doesn't exist. It never did.'

'The reason I—'

'You thought by marrying me you could force Jack and Jean to accept me.' Her arms snaked around her waist. 'What you didn't know at the time was that they already had.' Her mouth opened and closed, but no sound came out. 'And I have a feeling you'd never have proposed to me if you'd known that.'

'But you said I was yours.'

Sol smiled, but it didn't warm his eyes. Cassie shivered. 'You're not, though, are you?'

She had been when he kissed her. His and no one else's.

'What you did was kind and brave, but...' He reached out and brushed a finger across her cheek. 'I don't want a sacrificial lamb.'

He had to be joking, right? She was no—

'I don't want to look in your eyes a month, a year, or even ten years from now and see regret there.'

But he wouldn't, she wanted to cry out. The look in his eyes kept her silent. Pain she didn't understand razored through her chest, then pooled in her stomach. She didn't get it. She should be relieved—happy, even. She'd never wanted to remarry. So for the life of her she couldn't work out why her future suddenly stretched out before her to a never-ending horizon of grey.

'Still friends?'

The query thumped her back to earth. She lifted her chin. 'Of course.'

He didn't need her any more. The thought slow-burned through her. Sol had come back to Schofield to find out if he had a role in his family. And he did.

He'd used her!

Her stomach started to churn. He'd used her. Not that she blamed him for that, but it put an entirely new spin on the interest he'd shown in her. To think she'd thought…

She pushed it away. It had all been just a

dream—a fantasy. At her age you'd have thought she'd know better. But she hadn't lost anything, she reminded herself fiercely. The Parkers were still her fabulous family. With an additional member to swell the ranks. She was still the town's much-adored merry widow. Sol was still her best friend. It should be enough.

It would be enough.

Friends? She could do friends. She gritted her teeth. She'd do friends if it killed her. She slipped her arm through his and pasted a bright smile to her face, tried to ignore the jolt of heat that rushed through her at the contact. 'Let's go party.'

Never would she let him know what that effort cost her.

The moment they returned to the house Cassie dropped his arm and fled to the solitary seat beside Alec. She wondered if he felt as bereft as she did. 'How are you holding up?' She tried to keep her voice light, but a dead weight had settled in her chest.

'Good, lass.'

Then he glared at her, shifted in his wheelchair.

'You were right,' he grumbled. 'The Parkers are a nice mob. And Sol's a good lad. He deserves to have it all work out for him.'

'He does.' She eyed him for a moment. 'You're still the man who brought him up, you know. Sol will never forget that.'

'Aye.' He squared his shoulders. 'He told me he'd have to make do with two fathers. What about that? What do you think about that?'

She reached across and squeezed his hand. 'I think that makes him incredibly lucky.'

Alec squeezed her hand back and they both stared out at the crowd…and at Sol.

'Cassie!' Tracey glared at her, scandalised. 'You're not even ready.'

Cassie glanced up as Tracey tripped through the back door. 'Ready for what?'

'The nursing home lunch Sol organised.'

She knew that, but pretending to have forgotten seemed a wiser course than admitting she'd been sitting here brooding. And a whole lot wiser than blurting out that she wasn't going.

'Are you hungover?' Tracey demanded.

She drew herself up at that. 'On one glass of champagne?' She might not be much of a drinker, but…

'Well, why else would you forget about the lunch?'

Sol's New Year's Day lunch. Yesterday she'd thought it a great idea. Today all she wanted to do was sleep.

Tracey's eyes narrowed. 'Are you going to try and cry off? You can't, you know? It's all—'

'All what?' she sighed, when Tracey broke off and bit her lip.

'We only announced Sol as part of the family last night. We have to be there today to present a united front for him.'

'I don't think—'

'And if you aren't there it'll look like you disapprove.'

'Of course I don't disapprove.'

'I know that.' Tracey rolled her eyes. 'But nobody else will. Sol deserves our solidarity. The town cares about you, Cassie. What you think matters to them.'

Cassie's shoulders sagged. She knew it was true.

Not that the town cared about her *per se,* but they certainly cared about her as Brian's widow. She had to go. She rose with a sigh. 'I'll go get ready.'

Tracey followed her through to the bedroom. 'You can't wear that.'

Cassie stared at the navy skirt and top she'd pulled from her wardrobe. 'What's wrong with this?'

'Too drab.' Tracey took it out of her hands and shoved it back in the wardrobe before flicking though the rest of its contents. 'Here—wear this.'

Cassie swallowed. Tracey held out the pastel green dress Sol had admired in the shop window the night they'd gone shopping. The one she'd gone back and bought the next day. She shook her head and backed away. 'I don't think—'

'No arguing.' Tracey pushed it into her hands. 'It's gorgeous. You'll look fabulous.'

With a sigh, Cassie pulled her tee shirt over her head, unzipped her shorts and let them fall to the floor, then pulled the dress over her head.

'Gorgeous,' Tracey pronounced, zipping her up and turning her around to scrutinise her properly. She pushed Cassie into the chair at the dressing table and started pinning up her hair. 'Wasn't Sol fabulous last night?'

'Of course.' He was always fabulous. She roused herself. 'So were your mum and dad.'

'Lord, yes.' Tracey's fingers worked deftly. 'Mum especially. I don't know if I could be that gracious in the same situation.'

'They say love conquers all.'

Tracey's eyes met hers in the mirror. 'When are you going to tell Sol you're in love with him?'

Her jaw dropped. If she hadn't been sitting down she'd have fallen. She swung around to face Tracey directly. 'In love with Sol?'

Tracey sat on the bed, eye-to-eye and knee-to-knee with her. 'You are, aren't you?'

That was when it smacked her right between the eyes. She *was*. She was in love with Sol. It suddenly all made sense—why she'd asked him to marry her, why she'd been so happy when he'd said yes, why everything had become so grey and bleak when he'd said no.

In love with Sol. Everything inside her started

to sing. She'd been in love with him ever since she'd handed him a kitten out of the tree. Just like that. In the twinkling of an eye. Between blinks.

'But he doesn't love me.' The greyness shuttered back around her.

'How do you know?'

A ray of light glimmered through the greyness.

'You certainly won't find out by sitting here.'

Tracey was right. She swung back around on the chair. 'Make me beautiful,' she ordered.

Cassie searched for Sol the moment she burst through the nursing home's dining room doors. Her eyes lit on him immediately. How could they not? Sol had an aura that drew the eye like a magnet.

She paused, drinking in the sight of him. He'd dispensed with his normal cargo shorts and tee shirt. In fact he was more formally dressed than she'd ever seen him, and drop-dead gorgeous to boot, in a pair of sand-coloured chinos and a soft cotton dress shirt in the palest of blues. The strong breadth of his shoulders made her mouth water. The firm, lean length of his thighs made her knees tremble.

Yes. She loved him. Not that she needed any further proof. What she'd felt for Brian paled in comparison—the difference between a girl's infatuation and a woman's love. She wanted to give Sol all the love her woman's heart contained.

And she wanted to give it to him now.

As if he sensed her presence, Sol lifted his gaze. He gave a half-smile and a half-wave before turning away. Cassie's heart trembled. What if he didn't want her love? After all, he had said he didn't want to marry her.

No, he hadn't. He'd said he didn't want a sacrificial lamb. Her chin lifted. He had said yes that day in the tree house. Hope filtered through her, had her moving towards him. He turned his head when she was less than three feet away, though she had the strangest sensation he'd followed her progress across the room.

'Cassie!' He opened his eyes wide. 'See, Mrs Manetti? I told you she'd be here.'

'So you did, Sol. So you did.' She seized

Cassie's hand and pulled her down to the vacant chair beside her. 'I was just saying to Sol he reminded me of someone when I saw him on Christmas night, and you know who it was, don't you? Who he reminded me of?'

Cassie gazed at Mrs Manetti blankly, only half aware of her words as Sol excused himself and walked away.

'It was his father, of course. Jack!' The older lady laughed and gave a delighted clap of her hands. 'He's the spitting image of Jack at the same age.'

'Really?' She tried to inject interest into her voice as she watched Sol move through the crowd. She yearned to be at his side, part of the court that surrounded him. 'If you'll excuse me, Mrs Manetti, I—'

The older woman's fingers tightened around Cassie's wrist as she half rose to go. 'I've only caught dribs and drabs about the party last night, and I'm dying to know how Jack made the announcement. Did he do it in style? I bet Jean carried it all off splendidly too. But then she's a splendid woman, isn't she?'

With a sigh, Cassie subsided into her seat. It was pointless trying to fight it. She'd be trapped for at least fifteen minutes, if not longer. In normal circumstances she'd be happy to sit here and chat to Mrs Manetti for hours.

But today wasn't normal.

Cassie saw her chance twenty minutes later. Detaching her wrist from Mrs Manetti's fingers, she made her escape, almost running to catch up with Sol before he reached the swinging doors of the kitchen. As if he sensed her behind him, he turned, engulfed her in his smile, and swept her into the kitchen with him.

'I've found another willing volunteer.'

Jack, Jean, Tracey and Keith all smiled at her, all welcomed her noisily as Sol backed out of the kitchen with a *gotcha* twinkle in his eye. Fran waved from a seat in the corner, her status as heavily pregnant releasing her from any chores for the time being.

Cassie wondered if this was Sol's revenge for Christmas night, or if he really intended to avoid her for the rest of the party…the rest of her life. Defeated for the moment, foiled by his manoeuvrings, she returned everyone's smiles and with a sigh started chopping salad vegetables with Jean.

'You were right. He is a nice boy.'

Cassie stared at Jean blankly for a moment, then set her knife down with a clatter. 'I owe you and Jack an apology. I had no right to come barging in on you the other morning, telling you what you ought to do.'

'Oh, Cassie, you—'

'I should've known you'd do the right thing. I'm sorry—'

Jean pressed her fingers against Cassie's mouth. 'Never apologise for doing the right thing, my dear, or for urging others to do the right thing. I was so proud of you.'

Jean's outline blurred, and Cassie had to blink to clear her vision. 'You were proud of me?' she whispered.

Jean nodded. 'And it gave me hope that you could finally come out from the cloud you've been living under for the last eighteen months and live your life like I know you should. That maybe you could let yourself love again.'

Cassie grew aware of Jack, Fran and Tracey, all standing around her.

'And as a woman who loves you like a mother, Cassie, I'm overjoyed to see you embracing life again.'

Cassie couldn't say anything. She hugged her family and prayed that she could live up to their faith in her.

CHAPTER ELEVEN

SOL stared around in satisfaction. Everyone was here. And the meal was a hit with the nursing home folk—fish and chips and salad. The salads prepared by the volunteers in the kitchen, the fish and chips imported from two of the local fast-food shops.

Phase one was almost over. Phase two was about to begin.

He grinned. 'Phase one' sounded awfully grand for something that had merely involved getting a room full of people fed. Then again, it was more than that. Part of his giving back. He'd watched Cassie over the last couple of weeks, and she gave more of her time and energy and affection than any person he knew. It had shamed him. Today he'd given his money, his time and his effort to make sure the residents of the nursing home enjoyed themselves.

Now for phase two.

The corner of his mouth lifted. Cassie might feel she lived in Brian's shadow, might think she was only valued as his widow, but by the end of phase two she'd see how much she was loved for herself alone.

He glanced across at her table and his gut clenched. He'd almost blown it when she'd tripped into the dining room in that gorgeous dress. It skimmed her curves, outlining a shape burned on his brain. With her hair drawn softly back and the palest of pink lipsticks glistening on her lips, he'd wanted to stride across the room, take her in his arms and kiss her senseless.

Because she was his.

Then he'd remembered she wasn't.

But she'd made for him with such determination, and temptation had ripped through him so strong that he knew he'd never fight it—that he couldn't risk speaking to her alone. So he'd used her tactics and they'd worked. Maybe too well. She barely glanced at him now. A great gap opened up somewhere in the region of his chest.

'You'll be a fool if you let her slip through your fingers again,' Mrs Manetti intoned at his elbow. 'I know why you left ten years ago, Sol Adams. I know you young folk don't think we older folk have eyes in our heads, but we do. I know what you thought of Cassie…and I know what you thought of Brian.'

Sol shrugged. 'We were just kids back then, Mrs Manetti.'

'Yes, indeed. So don't go making the same tomfool mistakes now.'

Before Sol could answer Jean tapped him on the shoulder. 'Do you want us to bring out the desserts now, or…?'

'No.' He took a deep breath and rose. 'Let's get this show on the road.'

Cassie glanced up as a shiver of anticipation rippled through the room. Sol strode to the platform at the front and the crowd hushed.

'What's happening?' she whispered to old Mrs Crawford.

'Shh.' Mrs Crawford held a finger to her lips and practically bounced in her seat.

Heavens, by this time Mrs Crawford usually had her chin on her chest, and was snoring quietly. Sol must have something big planned. She glanced around the room. Was she the only one who didn't have a clue what it was? She swallowed. Nearly everyone's eyes were on her. She turned back to face Sol, and her mouth dried at the smile he sent her.

'There's an ulterior motive for why we're all here today, Cassie.'

There was?

With a grin Sol reached up, pulled a cord half hidden by the curtain behind him, and Cassie watched, gob-smacked, as a banner unfurled above him.

Thank you, Cassie.

She stared at it, blinked and rubbed her eyes, then stared again. She pinched herself. Nope, she wasn't dreaming. She glanced around to find everyone grinning at her. 'But...but it's not my birthday.'

The room erupted into laughter and

applause. Cassie sank down in her seat in bewilderment.

Sol hushed the crowd. 'Ten years ago, Cassie here was my best friend. I come back to Schofield after all these years and what do I find?' He lifted his hands. 'I find that Cassie is the whole town's best friend.

'Everywhere I go I'm told how wonderful Cassie is. Now, I know that, and you know that— but you know what struck me? That Cassie doesn't have a clue. She's too busy running around and looking after the town to realise how much she's appreciated, too busy helping a few elderly folk maintain their independence and stay in their homes a little longer, too busy making sure that those down on their luck at lcast have a full belly and a place to stay for the night.

'I left Schofield without saying goodbye. I left to make a better life for myself and I succeeded.' He paused, and his eyes gentled as they rested on Cassie. 'Cassie stayed, and she made a better life for everyone.'

Embarrassment flooded her at Sol's words.

She hadn't done anything special. She'd just been a good neighbour. She wanted to cover her face. She wanted the floor to open up and swallow her. But Sol continued on relentlessly, and the floor refused to oblige her.

'In other parts of the country on New Year's Day the Queen's Honours List is announced, to reward people for services above and beyond the call of duty. I vote we inaugurate a Schofield Honours List, where we say thank you to the people who make this town a fabulous place to live. And I vote that Cassie be the inaugural winner of that award.'

Sol stepped down from the platform and the dining room broke into a storm of applause. A lump blocked Cassie's throat. She watched in mute surprise as Jack got up on the platform and spoke about what she'd brought to his family, what she'd taught them about charity and kindness. Then a whole string of people followed—elderly folk she'd helped out, the director of the nursing home, the doctor. In fact it seemed that everyone she'd ever met wanted to get up and tell a story about her.

Sol had organised all this? Her eyes searched the crowd for him and found him leaning against the far wall, watching her. An odd smile played across his lips, and she understood his message. The town loves you, Cassie. *You.* Not Brian Parker's widow but you.

And for the first time she believed it. How could she not in the light of all this? A weight she hadn't even known she carried lifted from her. She felt liberated, free. Buoyant with joy, with life, and with the love she felt for these people. A love that she realised was warmly and sincerely returned. She hoped Sol could read her eyes. She hoped he could see her gratitude. She prayed he could see her love.

Keith's voice on the platform had her eyes slowly turning back to the front of the room.

'I always had the feeling Cassie thought I only helped her out 'cos she was the widow of one of my best mates.' He grinned down at her. 'Well, she was wrong.'

She was?

'Since our last year in high school, and regardless of whether she married Brian or not, I've considered Cassie a friend in her own right.'

He had?

'One afternoon at school she gave me a particular piece of advice that I remember to this day.'

She had?

'She probably won't remember this, but I was pouring out my heart to her because I thought I was in love with one of my mate's girlfriends. And I was full of it—*What should I do, Cass? What should I do?* She thought about it for a moment and said, "In five years' time who will you miss the most?"' Keith rubbed his chin. 'Got me thinking, that did. Nudged me right past the hormones. Since then Cassie's been like a sister, and that's why I look out for her.'

Cassie stared at him for a moment, amazed. And for a moment too overwhelmed to do or say anything. But his words bounced around her brain—who will you miss most in five years' time?

Sol. She'd miss Sol. In a blinding flash she realised it had always been Sol. She hadn't taken her own advice ten years ago, but she'd take it now.

Amid a storm of applause, she jumped to her feet and strode to the platform. Slowly the noise died down. 'I'm almost speechless.' She glanced around the room, trying to make eye contact with every person dear to her. 'At the moment my heart is so full I feel fit to burst. I don't think I really deserve this.' She held up a hand to silence the cries of protest that rose up around her. 'At least,' she amended, 'I don't deserve it any more than the majority of you in this room.

'All the things you've just thanked me for are easy for me because I have a little more time on my hands than most, and because your company and friendship mean so much to me. I want to thank you all for making Schofield home and I want to thank you for the honour you've done me today.'

She stopped, and the room broke into another storm of applause. As if on autopilot, her eyes searched out Sol. He grinned that crooked grin and her heart started to thump in her chest. She held her hand up for quiet, and slowly the room came to order again. 'Because all of you are my friends and only want the best for me, I'm going to share a secret with you.' She pulled in a breath, then plunged on. 'Ten years ago when

Sol left he took a little piece of me with him, and I'm not sure I've ever felt whole since.'

The dining room went deathly silent. Sol looked as if he'd turned to stone. 'The day before yesterday I asked Sol to marry me. At first he said yes, and then yesterday he changed his mind and said no.'

Gasps sounded around the room. Cassie almost laughed out loud when every head in the room turned to stare at Sol. Maybe she still had the power to gather a lynch mob.

She met Sol's eyes and held them. 'He said no because he thought I'd asked him to marry me to help smooth his transition into the Parker family. The crazy thing is it's what I told myself too. I told myself I could marry my best friend and have a family with him and make it all good between everyone.' She couldn't read Sol's eyes. 'I was wrong.'

His eyes dropped abruptly, and panic sped through her. She squeezed her eyes shut and forced her breathing to slow. She reminded herself she had nothing to lose and everything to gain. Everything.

She opened her eyes with a new resolve. 'I was wrong because there's only one reason you should marry someone.' She willed Sol to look at her. 'And that's because you love them.' Very slowly, Sol's eyes lifted. They were dark and deep and she wanted to plunge headlong into them. She lifted her chin. 'Sol, will you marry me?'

The dining room drew in a collective breath and held it. Cassie held hers right alongside it. Her heart plummeted when he glanced away. He thought she was playing games again. She plunged into the crowd, closing the distance between them until she stood in front of him.

'I love you, Sol. I don't know what to say to convince you of that. No man has ever made me feel the way you do, and it's not just physical,' she added when he shook his head. 'If it's not love how come I was so excited at the prospect of marrying you? And if it's not love how can you explain my wretchedness when you told me last night you'd changed your mind?'

She hauled in a breath. 'I know why you said no to me last night. What I don't know is why you said yes to me that morning in the tree house. If you don't love me I'll accept that. But if you're holding back because you don't believe me then I'll—' She lifted her chin. 'Then I'll have you up on breach of promise.'

A few smothered chuckles reminded her they weren't alone. A glint of humour momentarily lit Sol's eyes. She couldn't smile. It was all too important. 'Once upon a time you sat in a tree with me and held my hand because you knew I was sad. You always knew exactly what I was feeling. Back then you didn't doubt me. Why do you doubt me now?'

He stilled, and Cassie almost stopped breathing. Oh, heck, why didn't he say something? Her voice trembled. 'I can't help it, Sol. I'm yours, whether you want me or not.'

The air between them became so charged it wouldn't have surprised her to see sparks jump the distance. Such a short distance, but Cassie didn't know if she'd bridged it or not. She swallowed when he didn't speak, unable to read the dark depths of his eyes. 'You'd better say yes or no and put me out of my misery one way or another,' she mumbled, glancing down at her feet.

Suddenly he seized her hand and dragged her back to the front of the room, and onto the platform. He kinked an eyebrow at the crowd. 'Trust Cassie to rain on my parade.'

Cassie didn't understand the laughter that broke around the room. Several older women dabbed at their eyes with handkerchiefs. She smiled around uncertainly. 'What are you talking about?' she shot out of the corner of her mouth.

'This.'

He reached up and pulled a second cord, and another banner unfolded over the first.

Marry me, Cassie?

She gaped at the sign, then at Sol, then back at the assembled crowd. 'Everyone knew?'

Sol eyed her solemnly, then dropped to one knee and snapped open a small velvet box. Cassie gasped. A solitary diamond gleamed back at her. 'I love you with all my heart, Cassie Campbell. Will you do me the honour of becoming my wife?'

She choked back the lump in her throat. 'You love me too?' she whispered.

Sol rose, seized her face in his hands, and kissed her. For a moment she was too surprised to respond, then she threw her arms around his neck and kissed him back with her whole heart. She blinked when he finally lifted his mouth. 'Is that a yes?' she whispered.

He grinned. 'That's a yes.'

Only then did Cassie become aware of the storm of cheering and clapping and foot-stomping that had broken out around the room. Tears fogged her eyes. 'I think we can take that as approval.'

'And is that a yes from you, Cassie? Will you marry me?'

'I thought my answer had become a foregone conclusion.' She smiled, then sobered. Tears blurred the edges of her vision, leaving only Sol in her sight. She lifted a hand to his face. 'I love you, Sol. I want to be your wife.'

He slipped the ring on her finger, smiling, then his mouth descended towards hers. 'I'm all yours, Cassie Campbell. I always was.'

And his kiss told her he always would be. For ever.

* * *

Sol brought the car to a halt by the kerb. 'You're sure this is what you want, Cassie?'

'Positive.' She unhitched her seatbelt and turned to face him. 'I want to marry you, and I don't want to wait another second.' She'd already waited thirty-one days. Seven hundred and forty-four hours.

He reached across and kissed her. 'Amen to that.'

Cassie's heart knocked against the walls of her ribs. She wondered if she'd ever get used to his touch, or if she'd ever stop needing to touch him herself.

'What I meant, though...' he grinned his crooked grin '...is are you sure you don't want anyone else here?'

'The whole town witnessed our proposals. That'll have to do them. They'll understand.' She hoped. The town had gone mad—was talking about throwing some huge extravaganza that would take months to organise. There was no way on God's green earth she was waiting months to marry Sol. No, sirree.

He came around and opened her door without another word, his eyes bright with promise as he took her hand. As one they stepped towards the Town Hall—and as one they halted when the fire alarm in the building started up a high-pitched screech. They stared at each other, nonplussed, as office workers poured out of the building to join them on the footpath.

'Heavens above, Cassie and Sol.' Jill Crawford raced up to them, a pile of folders in her arms. 'I'm sorry, but I think we're in for a bit of a delay.'

'Is everyone okay?' Sol shifted, as if making to go into the building. 'Should I go in and check?'

Jill shook her head. 'We're well drilled. It's the third time it's gone off in the last month,' she said glumly. 'The system is old, and whilst we all know it's probably a false alarm you can't risk ignoring it.'

'Heavens, no,' Cassie agreed, trying to stifle the frustration that coursed through her. She shifted from one foot to the other. Jill was supposed to be marrying them in exactly twelve and a half minutes. 'How long do you think it'll be?'

'Took them four hours last time.'

'Four hours!' Cassie's shoulders slumped.

Jill eyed first Cassie, then Sol. She leaned in to whisper. 'Did you have your hearts set on being married inside the Town Hall?'

'It's not the where but the *when,*' Cassie blurted out. Man, oh, man. If she didn't marry Sol today then so much for being an old-fashioned girl, because she'd—

'How do you feel about getting married in the gardens of the nursing home? It's pretty in there at this time of year, and it's private too. Better yet, it's just across the road.'

Cassie clutched her arm. 'It'd be perfect.'

'Okay.' Jill unhooked Cassie's fingers. 'I just need to get my name ticked off by our fire drill sergeant, then we'll be on our way.'

Two minutes later she led Cassie and Sol through the side gate of the nursing home grounds, then around the back to where high fences guaranteed their privacy. A cheer hailed them the moment they rounded the corner.

Cassie stumbled. Her eyes bugged as she took in the assembled crowd. 'Did you do this?' she shot at Sol out of the corner of her mouth.

'Nope.' He rubbed the back of his neck, then grinned down at her. 'I think we've been set up.'

'You have.' Jill chuckled. 'Shame on you, Cassie. You know it's impossible to keep a secret like that in a place like Schofield.'

Sol laughed at her stunned face. 'Buck up, Cassie. Looks like we're getting married in style.'

His laughter washed over her like warm summer rain, and she suddenly found herself grinning back. They were getting married, and the where and the how weren't important. As long as she married Sol, that was all that mattered. And as she exchanged her wedding vows with him she was suddenly fiercely glad her friends and family were there to witness it. They were right. A wedding *should* be celebrated.

'Happy?' Sol asked several hours later, as he held her in his arms on the makeshift open-air dance floor.

The cake had been cut, the speeches laughed

over, the bridal waltz danced. Cassie wasn't sure if her feet even touched the ground as she was borne along on a tide of euphoria. 'More than I ever thought possible,' she vowed.

'I love you, Cassie Campbell.'

'Adams,' she whispered as the last of the sun's rays sank below the horizon. 'Cassie Adams.'

She swallowed thickly as his eyes darkened. She glanced around. The dance floor was crowded, the bar was crowded, and laughter sounded from all directions. There wasn't a private nook or cranny to be had.

And she was in serious need of a private nook.

'You know what, Sol?

He nuzzled her ear. 'What?'

'I think everyone has settled in to party all night.'

'Hmm…'

'Do you think they'd notice if we slipped away?'

He drew back slightly, stared down into her eyes, then sent her a grin that had the pulse racing through her body.

'Nope, I don't think they'd notice at all.'

Taking her hand, he led her off the dance floor and down to the back gate, where they slipped out quietly.

Of course the town noticed. You couldn't keep something like that a secret in a place like Schofield. But this time they all agreed. The youngsters had earned it.

MILLS & BOON PUBLISH EIGHT LARGE PRINT TITLES A MONTH. THESE ARE THE EIGHT TITLES FOR APRIL 2008.

THE DESERT SHEIKH'S CAPTIVE WIFE
Lynne Graham

HIS CHRISTMAS BRIDE
Helen Brooks

THE DEMETRIOS BRIDAL BARGAIN
Kim Lawrence

THE SPANISH PRINCE'S VIRGIN BRIDE
Sandra Marton

THE MILLIONAIRE TYCOON'S ENGLISH ROSE
Lucy Gordon

SNOWBOUND WITH MR RIGHT
Judy Christenberry

THE BOSS'S LITTLE MIRACLE
Barbara McMahon

HIS CHRISTMAS ANGEL
Michelle Douglas

MILLS & BOON®
Pure reading pleasure

0308 Rom LP

MILLS & BOON PUBLISH EIGHT LARGE PRINT TITLES A MONTH. THESE ARE THE EIGHT TITLES FOR MAY 2008.

————————— ✿ —————————

THE ITALIAN BILLIONAIRE'S RUTHLESS REVENGE
Jacqueline Bair

ACCIDENTALLY PREGNANT, CONVENIENTLY WED
Sharon Kendrick

THE SHEIKH'S CHOSEN QUEEN
Jane Porter

THE FRENCHMAN'S MARRIAGE DEMAND
Chantelle Shaw

HER HAND IN MARRIAGE
Jessica Steele

THE SHEIKH'S UNSUITABLE BRIDE
Liz Fielding

THE BRIDESMAID'S BEST MAN
Barbara Hannay

A MOTHER IN A MILLION
Melissa James

MILLS & BOON
Pure reading pleasure

0408 Rom L